"*Your book is not just a good book, but a great book!*"
Peter Apicella, NE Ohio

"*This book is rich in local history complete with thinly disguised names and locations and Indian lore ... I wonder if that Blue Heron that is squawking down at the river is a descendent of the one Dan includes in this story and is the woolen mill really the Dodd's Mill in Pleasant Valley?*"
J. David Ulrich, NE Ohio

"*This novel ... opens doors inward to the human soul and outward to a community of souls. From its initial beckoning, this carefully crafted story progresses enticingly to a soul-searching conclusion. From guilt to atonement on several levels, this tale needed to be told. It is of particular interest to those fond of history, archaeology or American antiques but of intense personal interest to those who have ever felt the need to forgive themselves.*"
Caitlin OCeallaigh-Walker , Baton Rouge, Louisiana.

"*This is a story of a man's redemption, both within and without, from the perception of his role in an historic tragedy. The book has a message that demonstrates the healing effect of caring, gracious people on a soul that undeservedly has been wounded.*"
Dana Flemming, NE Ohio

FACES

A NOVEL BY
DAN SAKACH

Innertech Publishing
Laguna Niguel, California

About the cover photo:
This face was carved on a huge rock on a steep cliff high above the Chagrin River. It has been dated as a late Whittlesley artifact from the period between 500 to 1300 A.D. At that time, Native Americans occupied many sites in Ohio between Battles and Rogers Road today. To safe guard it, the effigy was removed and placed in a private collection in the 1950s, where it remains to this day. Such faces were believed to have healing powers.

ISBN: 0-934917-01-9
EAN: 9780934917018
Ver: 1.2 - With author's corrections
Manufactured in the United States of America

To those who perished
As well as those who survived
And could never forget that day

Acknowledgements

Thanks to the following who contributed to help make this book possible.

The Cleveland City Councel and the Cleveland Public Library for their commemorative displays and enlightened programs during the centennial year.

To Authors:

Edward Kern, "The Collinwood School Fire of 1908," Cleveland, 1993

John Stark Bellamy II, for his enlightening essay, "Ash Wednesday Forever."

To the following institutions and friends who provided valuable information: Lake County Historical Society; Lake County Farm Park; Cleveland Metropolitan Parks; Rider's Inn, Painesville; Historic Sites of the Church of Jesus Christ of Latter Day Saints, Kirtland; Willoughby Hills Historical Society; Members of the Willoughby Hills United Methodist Church.

To the critical readers and hard listeners at the Standing Rock Poetry Group at Kent State University. And special thanks to friends for their critical suggestions, and to "Nonnie" who, after reading vast portions of the manuscript, introduced me with a vengeance to the Stanislavsky method of character portrayal.

To my brother Timothy Sakach, PhD, masterful editor of computer generated books.

To my parents Elmer and Marge Sakach, who grew up in Collinwood, where I was born, and who exuberantly provided more supportive stories than I could ever use. To Dad with whom I built my first hand-made cabinet; and to Mom, who, when I was a youngster, stood me at the rear door of Memorial Gardens, and introduced me to the names, and to that terrible big door that opened inward.

I made no fortune readers,
Had these pages storaged in a loft
Where rodents slept,
Until time again for your sake
And for mine -------
Opened words upon a page beneath a lamp.

Dan Sakach, 2008

Contents

Part One
New Faces, Old Voices

If there's no hatred in a mind,
Assault and battery of the wind
Can never tear the linnet from the leaf.
- William Butler Yeats

Chapter One

A Rare Find

SEPTEMBER 24, 2007

When Susan stepped up on the porch of Reed's Inn on the morning of her sale, the first thing she saw was her own face reflected in the sunlit window. It was a slightly contorted face, blurred in the dim light of the blown glass. She wore her Gucci sun glasses and sported a wide brimmed straw hat with a green ribbon that matched her skirt. "How grotesque!" was the first thought that came to her mind. For the first time, she saw herself not as an impressive diva, but as a ghost in swirling white and apple green colors. When she took off the hat and pushed the sunglasses onto her forehead, the image did not improve, for her eyes and lips spun about like debris on the surface of a flowing stream.

The glass was merciless. She fluffed her blond pageboy hair, and then moved closer to the dark window. When she smiled, her ruby cheeks puffed up as if they were balloons, and then she noticed a small embarrassing gap between her front teeth. The window magnified blemishes like one of those distortion mirrors at a circus. The bell tolled on her youthful vanity, but undaunted, she felt she could manage it. For this was the first day of her special antique show, and she was the best judge of her collection, and she knew something wonderful was about to happen. No contorted face, no amount of despair over aging could deter her. She stood straight up, threw her shoulders back, and looked beyond that contorted face into another face, emerging out of her soul; and there, like a still, small Yoda buried in a cave, her true self woke up.

For three months now, she was convinced that she had found the treasure of a lifetime. It was no ordinary antique, but a tall elegant secretary desk with intricate décor hand cut by a skilled craftsman. From the moment she found it, she believed that it was made in the eighteenth century, the golden age of handmade cabinets. There were only a few minor issues. She had no documentary proof to authenticate her claim. The man she hired for the appraisal seemed slightly unscrupulous. Then, there was this Mr. Hasseler who had a peculiar interest in examining this cabinet for "spiritual" reasons. And alas Paul, her husband, and her worst critic; on the first day of her showing, she knew if he even came here, he could drive her nuts. So, she stood firm in her belief in the cabinet, and moreover, she had a plan.

At this showing, Susan was determined to talk to everyone who came to see her collection. In her startling heels, wearing her favorite outfit, she would move like a butterfly, talk quickly like a bee. Even her smiles and frowns would be calculated. Lithe, petite, sparkling, at thirty one years, she knew how to spill over with excitement. When she smiled just slightly, her checks lifted up her eyes lids. At such moments, if her lips pursed just slightly before she spontaneously laughed, she could capture everyone. If this did not work, she would clasp her hands gently and listen intently to the guests. A firm handshake could win support from her worst skeptic. It was her big day! She was on stage, and she knew it.

The wide brimmed straw hat with a green ribbon that matched her skirt had always been a problem. Most of the time she held it in her hand, but outside in the sun when she put it on along with her sunglasses, she thought she commanded attention as she worked the crowd. But in her heart, she knew this hat was just a little over the top. So she might just quietly set it aside. And then there was the other problem. Reeds.

Reeds Inn dated back to 1812 and was somewhat gauche, but the curator had recommended it precisely because it was old, down to earth, all but profane, a subdued contrast to her joyful ubiquity. That was why he chose it, not her. For a moment, as she stood outside on the porch, she noticed the early signs of fall. The cool air. The few frail leafs that had turned brown. The dew on the grass. The eight white Doric columns on the porch. It resembled the porch at Mt Vernon, George Washington's home. It was believed that these columns were an innovation applied by a frontier architect not long after the Revolutionary War. This facade suggested that the rooms within would fit together in some sort of harmony. But that was hardly the case. The interior was chaotic.

Putting these concerns behind her, she turned, twisted the brass doorknob, and entered the main door and stood in a room that was once a small old post and rail building. She walked around and checked out the other rooms. For two centuries, this old house had expanded one way or another about every twenty years. There was a main dining room to the right, a smaller room with a large fireplace to the left, a kind of cozy bar to the rear, and. a large two-story wing that went off to the north. She walked through all these rooms and then went up the crammed stairway, where guests still slept in ten small bedrooms with four bathrooms. She smiled as she saw how the plank floors and walls in the hallways had twisted from extensive settling of the foundation. It reminded her of a haunted house. Reeds?

Somewhere behind and below this facade and its background, there was a kitchen and a partial basement. But she had never been in those rooms, but could easily imagine how crude and shabby they might look. Her curator friend told her not to worry; this Inn was blessed with a quaint sense of disunity. As she carefully descended the old stairway, her startling heels made sharp clogging sounds, reminiscent of a knock on a door. Fearful that she would disturb the guests who were yet sleeping, she removed these shoes and descended softly in bare feet. With each step, as the soles of her feet felt the worn stair treads, she felt as if she followed the pathway of a million mysterious travelers. Yes, this was the kind of contact she wanted. Arriving at the carpeted floor, she replaced the shoes and continued checking out the interior.

Around the corner in the main dining room, the desk itself stood near the door. The back was toward the door so that when guests entered, they would come from behind it and see dark, rough boards of poplar, very old and slightly warped. The base and top were two separate pieces which, when combined, rose nearly seven feet. It stood on a red carpeted platform that lifted it about six inches off the floor and allowed it to rotate. The roughness of its back stood in sharp contrast to its front. From behind, it was tall and aged like fine wine. From the front, it was an exquisite masterpiece. Showing the back first was an effect that the curator insisted upon, the stark image of fragile antiquity.

She looked up again at the unpolished truth on the back of that cabinet. With her finger, she touched one of those small hand forged nails such as were used during the colonial period. Then she traced a few of the gouges and nicks left by primitive tools. These things promoted the authentic value, but she knew some of these marks were last minute alterations by the curator. As far as she could tell, no one would know the difference.

When she circled around to the front, once more, she was astonished. Around its feet, a rippling bracket followed an exact outline. There were four graduated drawers, each one an inch narrower than the other. The contoured fronts of these drawers followed the prevailing motif of shells over columns. There were three columns all together. The two outside were convex, the center concave. This pattern repeated itself, only less pronounced, all the way up the slant top and continued up the vertical doors toward the crown. But the thing that caught her eye was neither the shells nor the columns, but the subtle marquetry composed of blossoms and leaves carved in unusual hardwoods. One hundred and seventy two of these tiny carvings covered her front. Even on that morning, this meticulous work entrapped her eyes because the overall pattern appeared to dance in a breeze almost like an exploding plume. Susan clasped her hands and murmured a short prayer. She planned for this day for almost three months now , and she was eager to share her excitement with everyone.

About an hour later, almost fifty people found their way into the dining room. They walked about studying over a hundred antique objects set out on display tables for sale. There were clocks and trays, jewelry, and old postcards. But everyone kept looking back and whispering comments about the tall secretary. It stood there as if it were a solemn bride, who had emerged out of the wilderness. Soon the curator arrived and stood next to it handing out his business cards and answering questions. Susan casually circled around the room explaining her collection of oddities, as she kept one eye on the crowd.

But then, there were the critics.

"So what's so special about this crate?" said Paul. He was a short, stocky man wearing a ball cap and slouching forward as he came through the door, looking first at the murmuring crowd then back at the tall cabinet. He wore a set of cheap, dark sunglasses that wrapped around his face like an astronaut's helmet. There was something ludicrous about the way his lower lip protruded as he carefully examined the cabinet wearing those sunglasses. When young, Paul aspired to be an engineer. After failing a few courses through an excess of partying, he became instead an auto mechanic. He succeeded in that trade through an internalized anger that said if one man made something, another could figure out how. But he carried this opinion to a higher level by insisting, at least verbally, that he could make any mechanical thing better than it was. This sentiment, of course, spilled over into the spiritual and political realms of life. Paul held an arrogant opinion about almost everyone, including God himself. It was his way of survival.

Standing before the secretary, he reached up to open the upper door.

"Sir, please do not touch the secretary! It's possibility two hundred years old and very delicate; and the oil in your hands could mar the finish," said Crandall Armes, the curator, He was a tall gangling man dressed in a sport jacket with a turtleneck. Crowned by a wide balding hairline, his face narrowed to a minimal smile on his thin lips which made it appear as if he just sucked on a lemon. A certified curator, he was naturally wary of those "bourgeois" types who unknowingly demeaned antiques. Something about the poorly timed grins, which blossomed forth across his face when others were unfairly embarrassed, revealed his self-absorbed narcissism. It was as if he took an excessive pleasure in discovering other people's faults. Crandall was no saint, but then again, he was meticulous. He was a true expert in dealing with this type of cabinet. He just pushed the authenticity card too hard, and this made Susan and others nervous.

Rather than disdain, these two men, actually, felt a mutual kinship in their irritation with each other.

"You don't say," replied the late guest as he squinted after removing his clumsy sunglasses and exposing the dark circles under his eyes. He shoved the glasses into his shirt pocket. "Yeah, well, I read that article in the paper. My wife's involved in this charade, you know. I can't believe this bugger. It's a piece of junk if you ask me!"

Suddenly Susan stepped quickly across the room. "Oh, oh, yes, Crandall this is my husband Paul. He's not seen the piece until now. He's not into antiques. So we need to fill him in on what's happening. How are you Honey? So glad you came to the showing," Susan, slightly taller than her husband , gave him a warm hug. "Isn't it marvelous that we found it! Oh everyone is so awestruck!"

"Nice carving. Nice inlay, but the backside looks like a barn door. Weird!" Paul spoke in a dour tone.

"Well, Paul, pleasure to meet you. I'm Crandall T. Armes, curator at the Winter Haven Museum. Here's my card. Do you understand the current value of eighteenth century cabinetry?"

"No, but I can fix your Toyota. I'm a mechanic!" Paul's sarcastic laugh fell flat.

"Well, my car is weathering well, but do not feel bad about the antiques. Not many people understand cabinets like this one, but allow me to explain some things briefly. I believe your wife has made an important discovery. Unlike the automobile, which is a product of mass production, eighteenth century cabinets like this one were built one at a time in shops where about five to eight craftsmen worked in a co-op. In thirty days with hand tools, they produced unique cabinets like this one over and over. Hardly anyone does that anymore. It's a lost art." Crandall spoke with the focused look of a stately owl perched on a limb. "Originality and economy were their twin concerns. To stay in business, they worked quickly. To please their clients, they produced unique objects. One of a kind."

"Yes, Paul, but we do not know this for certain yet!" said Susan, "When Mr. Hasseler comes here. I think he will provide a different story."

"We shall see, Susan, my research on this has been meticulous."

"But it could be a forgery!" said Paul. "That's what I've been thinking ever since I heard about this piece. Somebody could have pulled a fast one."

"That's not likely," said Crandall. "I have seen forgeries. They do exist. But there are tool marks and techniques, and moreover the design itself establishes a date. This is an original eighteenth century masterpiece! I know this for a fact."

"But the date is still being researched," said Susan. "We have not yet completed our research on the date."

"So what's the difference? An old cabinet's a cabinet," said Paul as he peered inside the carefully carved doors without touching anything.

Crandall raised his voice slightly and folded his arms firmly. "To put it succinctly, sir, the difference is perhaps one hundred thousand dollars. Maybe even more, if we take it to a New York auction house and can connect it to its rightful heritage."

"You're kidding me!"

"No, I'm not! That is why I stand here guarding it. We have people here even now who are very interested in this piece. It is an extremely rare find."

"A hundred thousand dollars for this piece of junk?" said Paul as he stepped back and began looking up and down at the cabinet.

"Dear," said Susan as she placed her hand on her husband's shoulder. "Keep in mind. We are trying to trace it to an historic family or a distinguished household. Such information could increase its cultural value immensely."

"One hundred thousand dollars! You say? Who owns it now?"

"Paul, dear, now slow down, and listen carefully. I tried to explain this to you last night but you fell asleep. You see, I, I mean , we own it. I bought it out of an estate sale three months ago."

"For what? What did you pay?"

She leaned toward him and spoke in a low whisper. "Five thousand dollars on my charge card out of my business account? Everything is OK."

"Okay? Holy barn boards! I'm the sucker who has to pay for this crate!"

"Sir, it could be a spectacular investment! Believe me! Your wife has made a genuine find."

"Now let me get this right. My wife, who owns this, is trying to knock the value down, while you want to jack it up. Is this what's happening here?"

"It's called the appraisal period. We are in mid stream on that," said Crandall. "We are in fact searching for more information about who the original owner might have been. That could change everything."

Paul raised his voice, lifted his hands over his head , as his turned about nervously. "No! Midstream? The ship sank three months ago! I've taken this cruise before!"

"Excuse us for just a minute, Crandall, " Susan said and she guided her husband toward the food tray , mumbling bits of conciliation and explanation. At this point, she began nonchalantly picking food off the table as she spoke in almost a whisper.

Crandall rocked on his heels as he concealed a subdued snicker.

Susan felt more than slightly embarrassed, as she held on to her husband's lapel, and spoke gently to him in a tender voice. "Now listen to me, dear," she said while she looked fervently into his eyes.

"I'm listening to this one. Is this like that broken down butler's dresser you bought last year?"

"Paul, listen. Last June, I was at this estate sale in Cleveland Heights. We were permitted to go into the attic of this old house. When I got up there, I saw a brown tarp over top this large object that was laying on its back. I pulled back the tarp, and took out my small flashlight and beneath a thick layer of darkened wax and dust, I saw those upper doors for the first time. As I studied them, I sensed something mysterious. I felt as if long ago someone poured his soul into that workmanship. I knew right then this was a treasure. I could feel it like a gradual blossoming rose. This cabinet was made by someone who... whose heart was strangely broken!"

Paul twisted his face and shook his head as he looked around the room before he looked back into her eyes. "I'm listening," he said in a quiet tone that imitated her conspiratorial voice.

Gently, she tugged once more on his lapel. "I sought for the owner immediately. Ziblowski was his name. He told me that years ago his grandmother bought it from someone for a substantial amount. He said to the best of his knowledge it was owned by someone in Lake County, but he had no idea why or when it was built. He said he was going to have it fixed up and appraised, but he had no time or money to do anything with it. So, we dickered over a price and I bought it for a fraction of what it was worth. Now listen to this."

"I'm listening. Sounds weird, but I'm listening."

"Among these people here today, there are some serious collectors, people who understand this kind of cabinet. Now I hired this man whom you just met. Let me tell you something. He's good, but he's too good. He makes me very nervous."

"How's that?"

"Paul, he took the secretary to a shop he rented, and he tampered with it. He took some boards off another old cabinet and put them on the back of this one. He said that someone had made small unimportant repairs to the original and he had to make them right again. But he told me to tell no one what he did. He said dealers do this all the time. He said it's an original piece as long as it's seventy per cent original. This one, he said, is ninety per cent untouched. "

"Oh boy! Maybe I better talk to him before we all get into trouble."

"No! Don't you dare!" she said in a long prayerful whisper. "Paul, there is more to this. He said during the sale we should take different roles on the disputed date. He will strongly advocate the 1770's , I 'm to cast doubt gently on this opinion. He said this will open up a discussion among the group that has come here. Paul , I have already taken care of that. You see Mr. Ziblowski said it was possibly owned a long time ago by some Mormons in Kirtland. He was not sure about this. I happen to do business with some of those people, so I called them. They had no idea of what I was talking about, but they connected me to this antique expert named Jeffrey Hasseler in Utah. He is a very old man. He is coming here. I talked to him on the phone two weeks ago; he said if it is what he thinks it is, he could positively identify a later date and the actual builder beyond any shadow of a doubt. But he needs to see it himself."

"Is he a buyer or just a looker?" Paul asked as he rubbed his chin.

"We shall see. He's a man of few words. I know that. He wants to see it. He called it a great act of atonement. Can you believe that? He would not tell me what that meant."

"For goodness sake, you can get into the middle of the weirdest things! Is the President coming with a bid from the Smithsonian? And don't forget the Pope? How about the CIA?"

"Paul, relax. Visit with people here, but do not, do not talk about the repairs. Not a word! We are waiting for Mr. Hasseler, who is on his way. So be calm and polite, and dear, I need your support."

"Support? Oh, no problem! I brought my wallet."

"Paul, don't be funny. This could be a big moment for us!"

So the elegant secretary stood there before the milling group of potential buyers, this tall bride in whom the sacred and the profane commingled as if poised on the brink of some sort of revelation. She too waited for that frail little man almost ninety years old who even now was in flight from Utah to Cleveland. In Jeffrey Hasseler's memory there was an answer;

not some secret analytical information about techniques and tools, but a story of pain and love and a courageous will to create. This story held the key to the cabinet's authenticity.

The people gathered at the Inn for the sale knew nothing of Hasseler's story. Susan alone had heard fragments of it. Crandall dismissed what she heard as nonsense. For like all stories, unless some teller cherishes and preserves the details , the tale itself will   sink into that black hole where essential facts vanish never to be retrieved. History is a record of eyewitness accounts passed along either orally or written down. When such accounts slip beyond the mind of those living, and the accounts have not been carefully preserved, then reality itself becomes cloaked in darkness. And once this happens, the truth may never again be known, unless, of course, someone comes forward with new evidence.

So it was, they waited for this one man.

Chapter Two

An Old Tool Chest

April 6, 1908

A long time ago , beyond the memory of anyone at Susan's sale, there was one willfully obscure man who knew something about the origin of this antique secretary, but his voice had been silenced for decades. Almost exactly a century ago, Ebeneezer Collard, better known as Ebb, stood in a cruder doorway and listened to different voices as he rubbed his right hand over the rough unpainted door jam of an original log cabin. The burn wound on his right arm had almost healed, so he did not need the old bandage. The gray-flaked wood on the jam had run its course. It needed to be replaced. He glanced over his shoulder at the ceiling beams that hit his head when he stood straight up. At that time, the cabin was perhaps a hundred years old, but it still remained strong and secure. Somebody had kept the roof from leaking.

Across the room, Jenny, his wife, sat in a dark corner and looked out a window as she rocked a kitten in her arms. In front of her on a hard bed, her exhausted eleven year old snored as he slept. She worried about him. At his age, the boy had seen more pain than most adults could bear. She prayed for him, as she stroked the kitten's back and glanced at the sunset.

Jenny was a meek descendant from a long line of tenacious pioneers. Born in a small town in eastern Pennsylvania, she was a quiet soul who parted her dark hair down the middle and often wrapped it behind her ears with a band or scarf. Her dark eyes darted quickly, but her thin lips spoke sharply. Her mother died shortly after her birth, which created one of those hushed, tragic memories that trailed her throughout her child-hood. She was reared by an elderly aunt known to many simply as Mrs.

Sparks. Her father was the blacksmith, sheriff, mayor, and regular ruffian to a town of about three hundred fiercely independent people half of whom lived in log cabins even at the end of the nineteenth century. As a teenager, Jenny worked on farms in the summer, tended school in the winter, and spent her free time sewing clothes, canning food, and cooking.

Throughout her early adult life, her uncle Henry watched over her with a protective eye, giving her advice, and often money, clothes, and food whenever she needed such. In 1897, she moved to Cleveland where she lived with her Uncle Henry and his wife Mabel. She worked as a seamstress in a factory. She met Ebb at a church picnic. They were married at the Collin Wood Baptist Church in 1897. Donny was born one year later, and then Salina came and sadly died in her first year. There were no more children after Salina.

All Ebb could see of her was a soft silhouette. She rocked and sometimes glanced out the window as the runners on the chair made a soft squeaking noise, a rhythm something like a distant drum. An eerie, disturbing sound.

"Hum! So this is it. This is the way its gonna be. God's country. Fine thing you done. Fine thing for your son. I liked our old window in Collin Wood just a tad more. At least, it weren't cracked."

He glanced sharply out the door, still scratching the dried wood on the weathered frame with his right hand. His name itself was as unusual as that stern face that hung over his injured soul. Ebb was abbreviated form of Ebby, a childhood nickname conferred by an older sister and later shunned in adolescence. His heritage was English, and the name Collard implied that his ancestors were entitled to some form of special benefit by reason of grace. He did not know much of anything about that. Any benefit by grace vanished a long time ago for him. He lived the desperate life of the working class. His hair was thick and raven colored and customarily parted down the middle. For years, he sported a small mustache, which he trimmed infrequently. His dark blue eyes darted around a room or launched into outer space and often captured the attention of those few who thought they understood the man. His face had a ruddy tinge, but could pale when he was exhausted. He had a stocky and tightly packaged body that loved a good hike. A careful worker in denim and red wool, he loved to swing an ax high over his head as well as to chisel minute designs in hard wood. But after the traumatic events of the past thirty days, he was just now getting back in shape. Only now some rage within him made him want to run harder than he ever had in his entire life. He tried to move beyond that rage, but the best he could do was subdue it. He was a man with many misinformed enemies.

A slight grin came across his face as he listened to his wife's grumbling that evening. His lifted his right eyebrow, as he was prone to do whenever he concentrated. He said nothing only listened keenly, not to her merely but for something to happen out by the road. He stared down the trail to where it turned between two stout maples and opened up on the gravel roadbed. The more she groaned on the squeaking rocker, the more he felt a sharp pain like a boiling kettle in his stomach. He felt an urge to run down that drive and up that hill, and to keep on going, maybe for a year or two riding the rails across the country, not going anywhere in particular, just going. But he had done that sort of thing when he was young. It never got him anywhere. It certainly would do no good now. So he stood firm, silently listening as he moved with slow deliberate gestures as hunters do when they stalk deer. Occasionally, he grinned.

"Yep," she said. "Fine thing you done for your son."

He looked to the right at a cornfield, with knee high stalks, brown and broken. To his left, a trail that went up into the deep woods. He loved the nested leaves and hidden crevices of woods more than he did the flat open field. The woods made him think. In the woods life was rife and rich, and older than any man's mind or dream; older than the Bible as far as he was concerned; older than language itself for that matter. Older than all those ancient and superstitious sputtering words spoken by any misinformed preacher. The woods were full of seeds, and had been that way for millions of years; and would remain that way so long as men did not intrude with their axes and fires. In the logs of the woods, the grain had those same kinds of whirling marks that you found on the palm of your hand. Finger prints. Hand prints. Wood grain. All alike, the prints spoke in one voice of a God who did not need to run away from anything. Not even a sputtering wife praying for a sleepy child in a squeaky rocker. So he said, "This here's a new start for us Jen. Things will get better. This place just temporary."

"If and when we get a nice place," she said, "You got to stop this grievin'. I can tell you even grievin' right now as you speak. I know you Ebb Collard. You don't hide much from me. Like Uncle Henry said, 'It's over now. Forget it and move on.' Scares me the way you keep grievin' for those children."

He squinted hard, pushed his cap back off his brow, and tweaked his mustache. "Aint grievin'." he said, "Just watchin' the woods like I done when I was kid. All that stuff! That fire. Those screaming kids. It's behind me now. No more turning back to that godless city. Never again."

"Don't you try to avoid it now," she said and raised her voice.

"Hush woman. Ain't grieven."

"Huh! Ain't grievin! He says! Ebb, I feels it sittin here."

Up on the hill to the north, he could hear the faint sound of a horse trotting at a brisk pace. He could hear a rider coaxing the animal. At first, he could not see them for it was nearly twilight. He squinted again and stepped out of the doorway so that he could listen without being bothered by her nervous agitating voice.

"Ebb, don't be ignoring me now. You know I mean business."

"I ain't ignoring no one. I'm just listen'. I think I hear Feargus. I believe it's him. He said he was comin' by on that big horse of his. "

"This late in the day?"

"Yep. I believe he's turning by the big maples, at a good clip too, right now. Our man is here."

The rider sat tall and proud on an English saddle, as the horse and he bounded in smooth rhythms like gentle ocean waves. He was a balding man with a handle bar mustache. In his left hand he had a small crop, which he did not use sparingly. His jodhpurs and black boots seemed out of place as he swung around in front of Ebb's lowly cabin and dismounted tying the reins to a small sapling.

"Great to see you Feargus. I was beginning to wonder if you would make it tonight."

"Great to be here. We had a late dinner back in the Inn at Willowford. Couldn't get away any sooner." Feargus Ware was a millionaire with the manners and demeanor of a man who was out to change the world. He had a slight English accent; his speech was quick and to the point. A visionary, he was that kind of man who made decisions that had historic consequences. He was the man who developed the distribution process for all oil refinery products. In a lifetime of errors, few men made the kinds of decisions he made every day. Feargus was a vice president at Allstate Oil Co, and for a decade he helped drive that company to a pinnacle of power and wealth so vast that even the United States government feared it and him too. Ten years ago, Feargus made one important decision that brought him here to this humble cabin tonight. In 1896, he bought about five hundred acres of the surrounding farm and woods, and he planned someday to build not another log cabin but a castle. As a recent part of that plan, he brought this broken man, Ebb Collard, here to the country to be his own private cabinetmaker and handy man. By sharing his dream of wealth, he hoped to heal the wounds of the Collard family.

The two shook hands and laughed. "How's the wife handling this? Should be warm and dry here."

"We fine. A little cramped, different from the city. But I grew up in the country. I like the quiet and peace. Makes her nervous. She favors city life. But we fine."

"Great. I had the mice and rats exterminated last week. Don't be alarmed if you find a few dead ones around. The cabin, Ebb, like I told you before, is temporary, just until we get the farmhouse fixed."

"We fine. We fine."

Feargus switched the crop from hand to hand as he talked and pulled off his leather glove. "Let me see the misses, for a second," he said. "Jenny," he shouted as drew close to the cabin door.

"I'm in here, Mr. Ware. I'm okay, it's just kind of dark that's all."

He poked his head into the room and saw that same silhouette that Ebb just studied. There was something portentous about her clinging to that kitten and watching the boy. It was as if the mother had seen some traumatic change come over the boy and she was deeply worried. He paused before he said, "Jenny, I know it's a little rugged here right now, but give us some time. We will fix you up with a lovely place and friends too. Everything is going to be fine. Right now, is there anything I get you?"

"Well, for starters, that fire wood has got to be cut down smaller to get in that iron stove."

"We will work on that. Tell you what," he walked over, opened the iron door, and looked inside. "Looks like you need something eight to ten inches long. I understand. I'll have the boys at the mill cut some first thing in the morning. Listen I'll have it up here by noon. I'll be checking on you from time to time. Write down a list of things you need. Give it to Ebb. I need to talk to him for few minutes, so you just take it easy. Have a nice evening."

"Appreciate it, Mr. Ware."

"Out in the country, we are all part of one big family," he said, as he walked away.

Feargus went back to where Ebb stood and motioned him away from the house where she could not hear their talk. He looked straight into Ebb's eyes. "Now, let's talk man to man. And you know what I mean to talk about. I ran into Stormy Wilson in Willowford the other day. He owns a small cottage on an acre of land just south of Willowford. These days he comes here on weekends mostly. He heard you were out here, but I didn't tell him where you were. He brought up that business about the school door, but I shut him down right off. Yes, sir!"

Ebb shook his head in an anguished outburst of deep denial, "No tellin' what all those folks might be sayin' about me now. They are all a pact of liars! Trust me! They're a lynch mob, especially those women."

"Now listen. Forget Wilson, and forget those people. Avoid him as much as possible. And forget the school door. We've talked about this before. The man is destined to make trouble wherever he goes. But I have friends working on this. They will get to the truth on what happened on that day, and they will make it known. There's a big investigation still goin' on. You and your family had best lay low here where no one can find you except me. This hideout is a safe place for you. It's all in the past, Ebb. It was an accident. The whole building was a firetrap from the start. Tragic indeed, but no one is to blame for anything that happened. I don't need to hear of it again. I brought you here because John D. himself said you were the best cabinetmaker he had ever known. I brought you here because I need you. I have big dreams for this whole valley. The future is bright with hope down here. So forget that that business. Do you understand me?"

Ebb looked directly into the man's eyes as never before. "I hear yah! But this thing ain't lettin go of me that easy," he said. "I know those folks back in the city. They're huntin' for me."

"Now, take your time. Healing takes time. Getting at the truth takes time. That fire will hurt us all for a long time, but we have to move on. You were telling me last week about some tools and a plan for something you wanted to build for me. I'd like to see what you are talking about. It may give us both something to dream about."

"It's all in that shed back behind the cabin."

"I want to see this now. I want to know what we are talking about."

They walked back to the shed. Ebb turned back the crude door and pulled out a lantern. He lit it with a match and hung it on the rafters. They went in. The place was damp and pungent. Feargus coughed and rubbed his eyes because there was a lingering odor of dead animal, probably a mouse. Ebb pulled off his cap and hung it on a nail next to the lantern. With strong and slender arms, he pulled an old tool chest from under a workbench and set it on top the bench. It was a six board chest made from hard maple. It had no feet other than wooden pads. It was about thirty inches long, eighteen high. The corners were hand dovetailed, but the dovetails were all different sizes as if they were patterns for different styles. There was a wrought iron lock and Ebb opened it with a skeleton key. "This here chest was my great grandfather's. He built cabinets back in Connecticut before the Revolutionary war. He probably came from England as a servant." Ebb lifted the lid back gently. It was supported by a hand made brass chain. Feargus moved closer and both men peered into the box. It was full of antique woodworking tools, hammers, chisels, fine thin saw, and robust hand plains, even fine brass hardware. All of the tools more or less custom made from metal and wood.

"When I was yet a child, my grandfather gave me this tool box. He said that in every tree you can find the hand print of God. He said cut the wood square and plain it smooth, and you will see the face of Jesus shining in the light of day, just as if he rose again. It was some sort of creed. My grandmother was an Iroquois. My family always lived close to the soil, even though they worked wood like New York cabinetmakers."

Ebb brought the tools out one at a time and handed them to Feargus who turned them over and over in the lantern light.

"These are vintage. I've seen things like these on display in London. This one here's a gent's saw, a Sheffield. Says right here on the blade. Ebb, these are worth some money."

"They are hard to use, too," said Ebb. "See here he shaped his own oil stones. Look at this hand plane. Custom made for a particular grip."

"Interesting. So what do you plan to do with these?"

"That's another story. The Koladari." Ebb pulled a folded parchment and laid it out on the table. In the upper right hand corner written in elegant script was that strange word. He pointed at it with his finger as he spoke. "This sheet has the design and dimensions for a fine secretary desk in the grandest style."

"Sure enough, Thomas Chippendale developed this style. George the First or Second I believe," said Feargus. "Desks like this can be found in most eighteenth century mansions. Amazing detail. Do you want to build this?"

"I'm saying to you right now, since I was a child, I wanted to build this with these tools, but I never had the time to even begin. I need a shop, a special kind of shop to do this. I'll build it for you if you want."

"I will get you set up. Just give me some time. A few months maybe. Amazes me that you even have this."

For an hour, the two men picked up those tools one at a time and moved them from hand to hand discussing their use. Tools in the hands of men are like seeds planted in the spring soil. Only in this case, the seeds are planted in the imagination. Fine steel blades and firm wooden handles inspire ideas of structures, designs. Dreams emerge out of dreams. But the time needed to direct the edge of a sharp blade carefully along the surface of hard wood is often much longer than the maker at first realizes. Things go slow. Things break down. Soon, the maker himself loses patience with his product, and abandons it in mid process. Besides that, life gets in the way. People run out of money, people get sick, people turn against each other, and the creative dreams whither on the vine. But neither of them thought about that on Ebb's first night in the country, as they savored the moment. Before Feargus departed into the night astride that big horse, he said, "That drawing gives us something to think about."

But for Ebb, much more was at stake in the tools.

Chapter Three

The Intent of A Soul

⧗

Back at the antique sale, it was now ten o'clock in the morning. Susan had managed to calm her husband down. He was naturally upset about the dubious value of the desk that he owned. This was to be expected. But by this hour, he had become curious about the enthusiasm among certain prospective buyers and investors. Seeing this interest grow, she decided that time had come to move the appraisal process to higher level. It was now necessary to provide some details and facts about old cabinetry in general and about this one in particular. She made arrangements for that. She had the group of fifty take up folding chairs and gather in front of the secretary to listen to Crandall. Paul sat on the front row studying this situation intently. A defining moment had come.

"As you all know," said Susan as she stood with folded hands before everyone, "I personally asked our friend Crandall, an authority on eighteen century furniture, to investigate the history of this secretary. In his research, he has found articles in antique magazines on similar cabinets. We have copies of those on a table by the window. As most of you know, most handmade antiques do not have dates inscribed anywhere on them. They were made by humble cabinetmakers some of whom could not read or write. So why should they put their name on anything? Also, they were often made in co-op's, which were small communities of millwrights, joiners, even blacksmiths, and woodcarvers who worked together on projects. So no one took credit for the project. Therefore, frequently with old cabinets, we don't know who made what.

"Also, I want to thank those of you who have purchased other items on display. Folks, just in case some of you did not notice, we actually have a sale going on today! If you find something you like, we are willing to negotiate prices. I do not want to haul all this back to my shop! So with that said, Crandall."

To be fair, we must note that Crandall had done his homework, but even so, there was something about his mannerism that aroused suspicion. Moreover, although the facts were few, the cabinet spoke for itself. He strove to elevate its value as best as he could. "Thank you Susan," he began humbly. "As Susan has just said, the origin of a handmade cabinet is perfectly foggy!" and with that he rendered that peculiar smile.

Everyone laughed, and certain investors in the room nodded their approval. "I want to thank all who are here for showing interest in what I think is an exciting discovery. Let me begin by asking a question. Has anyone heard of a man called Thomas Colladaire?" He raised his hand in a gesture of inquiry and looked around the room. The group gave a totally blank response. "Hum! No one. Not surprising! If it were not for two handwritten bills of sale, one for a lowboy and another a high chest, we would probably know nothing about this man. But in my research, I learned some facts about Colladaire. We know this. He apprenticed in a London cabinet shop in the 1750's; he settled with his wife who had two children near Hartford in the 1760's; he opened his own shop in Boston in the 1770's; he did some fine carving for families loyal to the King England, then disappeared without a trace during the Revolutionary War.

"These fragments of information, gleaned from a few bills of sale found in a drawer and some shipping documents, do not tell us much. For example, we do not know what he looked like. We cannot hear his voice. We have nothing written by his hand. We have no birth certificates. Of course, we have no social security records. No photo I.D. Not even any trace of religious baptismal records. Not having these resources is common in the eighteenth century. Tracing an obscure identity in that century requires more imagination than observation. Nevertheless, we do have five separate cabinets in a Hartford mansion showing this same kind of workmanship you find here today. The same identical tools marks, the same meticulous methods for carving and inserting wooden inlay, the same interest in lofty secretaries. All five cabinets of our find can be placed in the Colonial period, roughly 1770's. So that is what we know about him. As for this piece, we believe we have found his undiscovered masterpiece.

"Now as history goes, our evidence may not seem like much, but in fact, by any standard known to me, we have overwhelming evidence that he did this piece. In fact, it is my opinion this was something he sought to do all his life. This man strove to build more complex cabinets. I have slides and photos and measurements here in this notebook, which you can peruse later. You will see he loved marquetry and inlay."

For about twenty minutes, Crandall went on showing slides, drawings, comparing the cabinet in question to ones back in Hartford. Finally, after a fairly convincing presentation, he turned to the group and asked for questions.

Susan lifted her hand somewhat nervously, while her husband started shaking his head.

"Yes, Susan."

"Just so everyone knows. I personally found this cabinet in an attic in Cleveland Heights. Last June, there was an estate sale going on at the time, and this piece existed in two parts under a tarp in the attic. The owner had passed on and her son was selling everything in the house. In so far as this man remembered, this cabinet came from Lake County. In fact, the man was about to throw it out because he thought it was too crudely made. He was ashamed to show it at his sale."

Paul gave a burst of laughter, "Now, at last, a guy who makes sense!"

The whole room began to snicker and laugh.

Crandall tapped the table with his pencil. "Friends! Friends! In eighteenth century cabinets, rough workmanship frequently existed along side elegance. This was because the hand tooling was tedious; and if a structural part was not going to be visible, then the builders sawed and chiseled it as fast as possible. That was a common practice. It was a matter not of expedience and economy alone, but of craft. Valuable Time was devoted to areas where fine woodwork was displayed. The unseen areas did not matter. Similar practice can be found in furniture today. We must keep in mind carving by hand is a slow process."

The group expressed mixed reactions to this comment. "I've seen barn doors that were more beautiful than the back of that thing," said Paul and slapped his knee.

A man stood up, he seemed offended by the laughter. He was a silver haired man, wearing a fine sport coat and a large golden ring on his index finger. "My name is Bob Harper. I'm from upstate New York. I have a collection of these kinds of cabinets. I have bought and sold them for thirty years. My only comment involves the style and design of this piece. It's the late Chippendale. I want to make this clear. No cabinetry of this kind was ever made west of the Allegheny Mountains because, at that time period, this part of the country was the hinterlands, the wilderness. Wild Indians roamed here freely. This was tent and log cabin country, even as late, as say, the 1840's. So, from my understanding, it was never made in Lake County. Nobody had the time, the resource, or the reason to build something like this. I favor Crandall's opinion. This piece came from a New England cabinet shop of the 1770's!"

An irate gentleman sprang to his feet. "You missed the point. Cleveland, Ohio in the period from the 1890's through the 1920's was the center for some of the finest hand made cabinetry in the world, and after the centennial in1876's, there was a serious interest in making Colonial cabinets just like this. Wallace Nutting himself spearheaded that revival through authentic reproductions. So no, there could have been a man in this area who could have built this. Now if someone who knows this piece has suggested that it was made here, then, we need to know more about that. Yes sir, he could have worked for the Rockefeller's, the Hannas, the Halle's, the Garfield's, the Moore's and many others. Right here in Lake County! Those families had considerable wealth, and they employed some of the greatest cabinetmakers of that era."

The two men began quarreling. Soon others joined in, adding to the confusion. The group split right down the middle. Susan became alarmed. Her make shift jury of homespun experts seemed about to return without a verdict. So, with determination, she stood up and raised her voice above the dirge of voices, "Friends! My friends! That's why we are waiting for Mr. Hasseler. Before we jump to conclusions, we need to hear from him on this issue. He should be here this afternoon. He had a flight out of Utah, this morning. He claims he may provide an absolute date."

Amid the din, an older woman, who had the distinction of high school teacher, rose to her feet and said, "What we need to know is the motive for doing this? What was the intent? That is what I want to know? The intent of the cabinetmaker?"

Susan reaffirmed this by saying, "That's an appropriate question. I assume you mean for whom was this built. What family? What occasion?"

"Yes, that's exactly what I mean. Things like this were made for special occasions. A wedding perhaps, or the building of a new home."

"Crandall, do you have anything on this?" Susan said.

The man took a long time to respond, and then he said, "Ah, most likely, this belonged to a family that was loyal to King George since this is the Colonial style, but we cannot be certain of that either. At the time, this was the new and latest style. Very popular with everyone. During and after the American Revolution all this changed, of course. The Federal style became the new style in the early days of United States, when Washington was President. And as someone mentioned, after the centennial of 1876, there was a renewed interest in colonial antiques. Now what that means is that some old things were pulled out of the barns and attics and restored. That is extremely important point, because this could be one of thousand of restored antiques."

Finally, another man stood up. "I'm curious about the fact that somehow the Mormons were involved with this cabinet. Their Great Pentecostal period extended from the 1830's through the 1840, before the majority of them were forced to leave for Nauvoo. When they built the Temple in Kirtland, they had a mill, a cabinet shop, and they hired many skilled cabinetmakers. That was around 1836. Now, has anyone looked into that period? This would not be a likely project for the Mormons of that period because it is a little over the top on the stylish side. Mormons were basically farmers and humble tradesmen. Why have the Mormons been linked to this cabinet anyway? What is it with this Hasseler fellow?"

"We're going to learn that this afternoon. Trust me. We will learn more on that soon," said Susan.

At this point, Hasseler's absence became crucial. Paul shook his head and laughed. Crandall Armes rolled his eyes back, and folded his papers carefully as he looked down. The word "forgery" surfaced among some disgruntled mumblers in the room. Patience and prayer dwindled. It would require more than mercy to get this matter straight. What was needed were some simple facts about the intent of a soul. But what soul? Whose soul? If someone came along and built this in Lake County, that person must have disappeared a long time ago; usually when that happens, the truth dies with that person. So where do we go to discover a soul's intent?

"Who was it intended for? That's my question," said the disgruntled schoolteacher in the third row.

"Thank you for that question," said Susan. "Intentions are decided by a jury, and at this point that jury consists of all of you. So we need your thoughts and prayers. But our primary witness has not yet arrived, so we need your patience." Susan looked at her watch and then at the group. Her hopes for a big sale began to wobble. Perhaps her entire venture was premature, but she lifted her head with fearless pride. "Are there any more questions? If not, feel free to browse. As I said before, we actually have other antiques and collectibles in the room, and we will negotiate," she said.

"One question! Where's Hasseler?" said her husband as he stood up. Everyone laughed.

"Thank you dear," she said. "My dear friends, I go back to the moment when I discovered the meticulous workmanship which you see before you. Someone poured out his soul as he made this masterpiece. Let us all focus on that. For in that is the intention."

The group disbursed, and Susan donned her big hat and diva sunglasses and summoned her husband outside to the far end of the porch where no one could see or hear them. "Okay," she said as she strove to calm down her jittery stomach. "I have gone to great trouble to bring this group together today. It took time, it took patience, and it cost us money. Us! You are going to have to change your attitude or leave. Right now, I do not care which way you chose to go."

"It's just an old wooden crate!"

"That's not true! I grew up around woodworkers. My father built cabinets as a hobby. I have examined museum pieces. I know a masterpiece when I see one. I known what it takes to do fine carving and inlay by hand. I have tried to do inlay myself. It's tedious. And I want you to understand this: My group, this jury has come here today surging with excitement. I feel it. Some one is about to make a substantial offer. Now stop being the classroom fool! Stop undercutting me. Shape up or get out!"

"Ah, I get it. I get it." Paul said humbly as he shook his head.

"There are voices in my head, Paul! I hear them! There is a lot of screaming and crying. That cabinet is about to tell its own story! Start listening to
it! I'm telling you, listen with a sincere heart, if you have one. Am I understood?"

"Well, let me explain the voices I hear. I know this much about antiques. The great treasures do not get abandoned so easily. They go from
the mansion to the museum."

"That's not always true," she said. "Sometimes, they are misunderstood.
They need to be rescued."

Paul shook his head and looked into his wife's eyes. She was on a mission all right. "Yes, dear," was all he said.

Chapter Four

The Remote Farmhouse

May 13, 1909

One day, lost in time years and years ago, Ebb was startled by another voice. It was a man shouting to him. "Hey you? Ain't you Ebb Collard, the great cabinetmaker? What are you doin' down in that hole?"

Ebb heard the voice and looked up at the blinding light of the noon sun that glared like a torch. "Who's that I hear?" he said as he squinted and wiped his brow with a red bandanna. The voice resonated but he could not see the face because of the glare. It made him angry. When he worked, he worked intently like a steam-powered machine. He disliked it when someone threw him off from his concentration.

"It's me Elmer. Elmer Rodell! Remember me?"

"Not exactly. What brings you out this way?"

"I met you years ago when you built that big book shelf for The Mather Mansion down on East 25th street. Remember I was a frame carpenter on that house. Remember me?"

"Vaguely? So what brings you out here to the country?"

"I live out here now. I live on River Road right near Willowford. I'm working on these big country estates just like everyone else."

"Well, if you don't mind, I'm puttin' in a cistern. Our well don't serve us too well in mid summer. So I'm puttin' in a cistern to store water. I'm fixin' it so it can store run off. I'm goin to brick it up next week. Don't have time for visitors."

"A cistern? You shouldn't do this alone? ! I hope you know you're right close to killin' yourself!"

Ebb threw aside his shovel and looked around. It was hot. This was dirty hard work. It was the kind of work he hated, but he had to do it, and do it alone at that. He was standing on loose shale almost twenty-five feet down in a conical hole. He had a block and tackle hooked to lift buckets of dirt out of the hole. He could hoist himself up if he had too. Besides the hoist, he had a ladder by which he could climb out. So what did this fellow want? Ebb grew up in the country, and there he had learned independence and self-reliance at an early age. He resented any form of criticism. So he started up the ladder talking quickly in a firm tone. "I need water in summer, and this is how I'm goin' to get it. It's not a well, but a cistern. It's collect rain water from the roof."

Elmer chuckled. "You said that once already, fella. I say you shouldn't be doin' this alone. A couple of years ago, a fellow started diggin' one of these cisterns by himself and the slag broke loose. Took us four hours to get his body out once we figure'd where it was. Happens fast! I was there. It was a nasty sight."

When Ebb got to the top of the ladder, he stopped and took a breath. Before him he saw the smiling face of a strong man with dark wavy hair that fell over his eyes brows like hay in a loft. He had seen that face before years ago. Those deep gray eyes spoke of an alert intelligence. He shook his head and said, "I got this figured out pretty well. Don't need advice. Don't need help. Throws me off."

"I know what you mean," said Elmer. "Still around here folks like to pool their resources. A good draft horse might help you move that dirt faster. I can get one of those here along with some ropes. Ain't no use in killin' yourself."

Ebb stepped off the ladder and walked over where he kept a jug of cool water in the shade. His mustache and his hair dripped with sweat. His harsh angry tone spoke of one who liked to work alone no matter the price. "A fella would have to pay somebody. I can't afford that."

"You don't have to pay. It's different when poor folks pool their resource and cooperate. That's the way we do things around here. I mean folks from the church do things that way. Me, for instance, I would be interested in some of the stones you might turn up down there. Specially those bright crystal ones. The seer stones. They sometimes have power to heal wounds. I'd dig here for free just to search for one."

"Church, you say?"

"Yes sir, we are part of the Mormons! A small part. The Community of One."

'They the ones that built that temple up on the hill on Chillicothe Road."

"Yeah, that was the other part of us. The Mormons."

"Impressive building. Then they moved out west."

"Most of them left in 1839. Had a rough time too. But some of us never left this area. I could get you a crew out here. It makes things go easier for you. It might be a blessing to you."

Ebb turned his back to the man and looked toward the rolling field in front of his farmhouse. "I come out here in 1908 to get away from people. I don't like what happened in Cleveland a year ago. I don't like what people said about me and my family, and I don't even like civilization. These days, the wilder it is, the better I like it. If I die out here diggin a hole, I will die a happy man. I work for Mister Ware anyway. Last year, we lived in an old cabin in the valley for two months, before he got us this old farmhouse. I kind of enjoyed that cabin. Wife hated it. Anything I need he could get for me. Not that there isn't a price, but he and I work things out. Don't need no help. "

"Feargus Ware! He has no roots here! I know that man. He's not goin' to be here long. His wife and those fancy daughters of his hate that big farm he built across from mine. I was there puttin' up fence for him a few years back. That man's a dreamer. Why would anyone build a stone house that looks like a castle near Steele's mill? Don't make sense."

"Seems to me you know something about everyone," said Ebb as he scooped up a cup of cool water and poured it over his head. "You ever heard of the Lost Nation?"

"You mean the Lamanites. Sure, they broke away from the God of their fathers, and became violent people. It's in the The Book of Mormon."

"No I'm talkin' about the Erie Indians who lived in these hills three or four hundred years ago. They could hunt, they could fish, and they could make all sorts of tools out of stones and wood and leather. They could survive in tents and huts made from branches right out in the woods in mid winter. Make a fire without a match, too. Anyway! That's me. Wife don't like it too much, but I do. That's the way I want my kid to grow up. Don't need civilization. Rich folks and others with book learnin' bother me. Freedom, that 's my goal back here on the edge of the deep woods. Feargus ain't goin no where. Why the man owns over five hundred acres. Prime land too."

"Well, Ebb, sounds as if you are set in your ways. We in the church, well, we pray for people like you because the Bible tells us your way of life is dangerous. You need a community. You do as you like, but we're around if you need us."

"The Erie, The Cat people as some calls them. I've read a thing or two about them. Sometimes I think I am one of them! Ah EE! Mishkah!! I found traces of one of their camps right over there on that ridge. I found arrow heads and spindle stones and a big stone knife! They knew the land better than any white man. Sometimes, I think I hear them at night whispering and singing, Ah EE! Mishkah!!" He shouted and waved his fist at the sun.

Elmer stood up and looked at him with a cold stare and shook his head, as if the man were plum crazy. They talked for a few minutes about Erie Indian campsites. There were numerous sites in the area, but no white man ever met an Erie. The Iroquois killed most of them and drove the last remnant south around 1640, long before Europeans arrived. As he started walking toward the horse and wagon that brought him out to this edge of the woods, Elmer said. "My wife's part Cherokee. Her grandma on her father's side was full blood. I mean you can't tell the difference by look-ing. People are people as far as that goes. But family life, church life that's where we find hope and love. Out here alone like this. That's scary. I'll see you around my friend." He mounted his wagon and started turning it around as he looked back with a twisted lip.

Ebb did not say a word as he stared with a hard, long stare watching Elmer leave. When he was down the road a piece, he laughed to himself. "Guess I scared that fool off," he said.

He looked down at his hole as if it might indeed become his grave. The dirt lying out in the sun began to slip bit by bit back into the hole. That Elmer was right, he thought, as he watched the man roll down that long narrow trail that led to the road. Small bit sliding was innocent enough, but the weight of the mass could tilt over the edge and fill that hole in the blink of an eye. So he took a hoe and spent a few hours opening the rim of his hand dug well.

After this, he laid down under an apple tree and dozed off in the shade. There, he had one of those painful dreams. In that dream, he heard voices.

He was in this big mansion on Euclid Avenue. He was hard at work on a bookcase that surrounded a stone fireplace. He was building it for the Mathers, who owned ships that carried iron ore. He had a stack of quarter-sawn red oak that he had planed and cut to size. The ceiling in that room was over ten feet high, and that shelf rose to seven feet. He needed a ladder to top out that project. There were four windows along the north wall. Outside, he saw lush green maple trees and a garden with a trickling fountain. He watched as kids dashed around the flowers chasing hoops and riding bicycles. It was a wonderful happy place. Not that Ebb was rich, but the owner of that house was very rich and that meant Ebb had a secure job. There was a man there called Josh. He was spare and a few years younger. He had blond hair and freckles. He worked on the kitchen. It was lunch time, and the two men talked as they sat on the stack of boards.

"So, you live out in Collin Wood."

"Yeah," said Ebb, "we are about three blocks from the lake right near the boulevard and Euclid Beach."

"Got any kids?"

"The one boy. He'll be three years old. My how time flies! How about yourself?"

"One girl, Amanda. She'll be turning two this year. Been a rough year for the wife and I. Bringing up a kid costs some money."

"You hit the nail on the head there!" said Ebb.

"We live in Collin Wood too. One block off of Waterloo Road. I like it out there better than Cleveland. Taxes are lower, and rents affordable. Plus, we can take the streetcar most anywhere we want to go. Makes life easier. Now that they built that new elementary school, we think we might just stay there for a long time. And then there's the Lake. Wife and I met at Euclid Beach. Amanda's a little too small, but we take her down on the beach. You know kids. They love to run in and out of the waves, and once they get used to it, they cannot get splashed enough. But you got to watch 'em."

"Oh, you bet. My son loves water. I'd swear, he's part fish! But it's dangerous. That Lake is full of surprises."

"You know, we should get together some weekend. Have a picnic at Euclid Beach. Oh, let me tell you the best part of the Lake is watching that sunset. Oh that's peaceful. That orange ball settling into the blue horizon!"

"You got that right," said Ebb.

"Will your kid being going to the School?"

"Sure. We want to start him when he's six. But we already take him by there. "

"Well, we will probably be seeing a lot of you over the years. Here's my address. Let's plan on a weekend on the beach. Bring some friends. See friend, my wife's a country girl, and kind of shy. So you know, I got to get her out of the house."

"I know exactly what you mean. Mine's been a city person for years. She don't take an interest in country things. As for me, I was born and raised out in Geauga County on a big farm. I miss huntin', and fishin', but farm work you can take it or leave it. My family's always been in carpentry and cabinetmaking, for generations as far back as I know anything. So two years ago, I moved near Cleveland to find work like everyone else. Collin Wood is about as close I care to get to the big city! I mean to say, this is the place to be if you need a job."

"Oh yes, jobs everything. Plus you got the streetcar. It'll take you anywhere in less than an hour," said Josh. "I mean they got interurban in the country, but that's one line, you don't want to live too far away from it, cause if you do, you better have a good horse and place to keep the horse!"

"You know," Ebb said, as he stood up and stretched. "We should get together. Hey! Who's to say what the future holds. Why my son and your daughter will be schoolmates pretty soon. And well, let's just leave it at that."

"Leave her be as God and nature wants her to be!" said Josh as he slapped his knee.

With those promising words, Ebb's dream shifted violently. He was back at the fire.

"Where's my Amanda?" A voice shouted. "Where's she

gone? Amanda!"

"I seen her go back into the building," a little girl said. "She said she had to get her cousin out of there, said she saw her cousin in the window on the second story. Then she ran back in the building."

"Oh my God!" said the woman.

It's just as I said it would be. Its just what I feared. Those doors! Those big heavy doors! If only the kids could have pushed them. If only they could have broken the latch and the lock, and then pushed them, then this would have never happened. One stubborn man insisted that those heavy doors should swing inward. Who in the world would do that?

NO. NO. NO. That not true, said Ebb.

FOR EVERYONE WHO KNOCKS, THE DOOR WILL OPEN.

OPEN OPEN OPEN OPEN OUTWARD INTO THE WIND

Ebeneezer Collard, bow your head low in my presence, for I am that I am. Why your only son was there on that dread day! Are you not a most deceitful man? Because of this horrible action, I sentence you to death by burial in an open pit. It will not be painful enough. If you want to atone for this, you gotta pay somethin more! Paysomethinmore! Paysomethinmore!

But Lord, have mercy on me a sinner, for I was not the one who caused this!

Death by burial alive! It will not be painful enough! Paysomethinmore!

But what shall I pay? Do not leave me buried like this! Come Soon, O Lord! Come soon!

Around four o'clock, Ebb woke up confused and frightened. For a moment, he thought he was dead and buried in a pit. He put both hands to his hot cheeks and felt alive. He looked around as if he were in another country. Then he heard the voices.

Jenny and Donny had come back from town on foot carrying sacks of groceries. He could hear them talking in the house. He got up, shook his head. "I'm cracking. I'm going nuts," he said. He stood on his feet and dusted himself off. "Got to get my mind together," he said as he slowly walked toward the house. "Got to get it together!"

At the house, he heard Jenny complain to Donny, "Every time you go to town, you pay something more for things! Pay something more!"

When he entered the house, the screen door banged behind him. He stopped because it startled him. He felt deeply disturbed by this foolish intensity of his own nerves, but he would never tell anyone about it for fear they would think him crazy. He could not figure out why he was so disturbed. He did not say much just walked over by the sink and poured some kernels of seed from hand to hand, as he listened to his wife and child talking.

Jenny talked excitedly about her visit to town; then, she paused, turned around, and watched him with that kind of intention only a wife has. "Ebb, what happened? Why you got that expression on your face? I know what it is that does that to you. It's that business about those kids again, ain't it! You got to forget that. It was not your fault. You been grievin' again!"

"No, wasn't that," he laughed and shook his head. "Fella came up here talkin' about the Community of One Church. I knew him from Cleveland. He brought back some old memories from long ago. I think he wanted to make a few bucks, but I drove him with one of my Erie Indian stories. Nosey guy named Elmer. I run him off."

"Well, I know his wife. He's one of those Mormon folks that lives on the hill above the river. They have two boys about Donny's age, and a sweet little girl. Them and the widow Hasseler were down at the store in Willowford shopping for clothes. Nice folks. Fact is their ancestors started their church, wrote some of their own Scriptures and Songs right there in that Howell's grocery store down by the mill. They explained that to me just last week"

"Good for you. I heard all about it. You know I don't need a bunch of pious busy bodies comin' around botherin' me with religion when I'm working my farm. So shut up about those people," he said firmly.

"Well maybe I need friends! And don't be tellin me to shut up!" she retorted just as sharply.

He walked into the living room carrying a local paper that they brought from town. He sat down and read it. He felt dizzy. His head spun as if he were trapped in a smoky room.

So it was that he and his wife and the child slowly began sinking deeper and deeper into an empty hole of isolation on the edge of the deep woods. Feargus had rented them an old farmhouse with a barn and a stable. But it was off the main road in a remote location, and kind of shabby from being abandoned for about twenty years. They were there to restore it to a decent place. The rent was modest, but this project would take many years.

It all began with a choice he made to leave the city behind. For a summer, they endured the cramped quarters of a hideout in an the old log cabin. Then after they helped Feargus put a roof on a farmhouse, he rented it to them. Soon, life changed as the household chores mounted up. After digging the well came the plowing and planting. After the crop came the leaky gutters. One thing after another compounded his chores and took up his time. His secret dream of building some sort of exquisite cabinet in the stable behind his farmhouse made less sense everyday. Still, when things slowed down, he walked back there and pulled out those antique tools just the way he and Feargus did on that first day when they came to the valley. He turned them over in the window light and sometimes even sharpened the cutting edge on an oilstone. It was as if some voice in his soul called out to him from beyond this world. But over time, this voice shriveled up little by little like a flower plucked from the garden. The more that flower withered, the more bitter he became. It was the past that was catching up with him. It came after him wherever he went, and when he slowed and started to relax, it crept into his dreams and memories and thoughts like a serpent hissing and showing its ugly teeth. Not long ago, Amanda and Donny were two infants chasing each other in and out of the waves of the Lake. They had only begun to live. That was such a happy time, and in a flash, it was over.

He worried about Jenny and the boy. She learned how to live a hard life in an unpleasant way. Farming meant long hours of hard work, you never caught up, and almost everything was half done when you gave up on it.

But seeing that her friends from the Church brought her rewarding happiness, Ebb moved out of her way as best he could. She was a city woman in the country. She needed friends.

As for Donny, he learned early how to get out of work and roam at random through the countryside. He grew wilder by the day. The wilderness fostered an infinite freedom within him, and he loved it. Out of anger perhaps, or maybe out of flight from his memories, he ran with an abnormal passion. He held his head high, pushed his lower lip out, and teetered out of control. As he sky dived through life's experiences, the adults worried. Not if, but when would he crash?

Chapter Five

The Incisions of A Chisel

Back at the Inn, it was lunch time. Susan became seriously defensive. Some of the antique buyers left fearing a fraud, others came into the dining room where a small soup and sandwich buffet awaited them. The people scattered around the room made for some exciting chatter and laughter, but still there was no sign of the mysterious guest from Utah. She sat at a table with Paul, Crandall, and Mr. Harper, the man with the big ring. After some small talk about each other's backgrounds and affiliations, the conversation turned once more to the secretary.

Paul opened up a conversation with one of his typically blunt questions, which usually made her jittery. In his own mind, he actually tried to be sincere, but he had limited talent in the finer arts of conversation. "So, tell me, Crandall, you've been in this antique business a long time. What sort of mysterious expertise will we hear when this Hasseler fellow arrives?"

"You know, that's a good question. One issue that disturbs me is the fine inlay on the upper part of the doors."

"The small flowers!"

"Yes. That kind of woodwork requires some unusual woods gathered from a variety of sources most likely over a long period of time. The techniques and tools used to do this are difficult to understand. I mean the rest of the cabinet shows conventional dovetails and mortises, which, while the product of a skilled cabinetmaker, do not have anything unusual about them. As for the marquetry, well, it will surely be the key to defining who made it. To be honest, in cabinets built after 1800, I have not seen anything quite like this. Someone prayed hard when they built this one."

Susan's eyes dilated with approval.

Paul smiled quietly. "Maybe Hasseler has the tools," he said.

"That's very unlikely; however, he could," said Crandall. "What do you think, Bob?"

Bob Harper was a silver haired fellow who wore a plaid sport coat. He appeared refined, dignified, and perhaps wealthy, if a curious gold ring means anything. His age and wisdom seemed to become clearer as he spoke in a calm voice. "My years in the antique profession tell me he will not bring much of anything, nor will he change our opinion. These old eighteenth cabinets are not that hard to recognize. I think if you put fifty of them in a gymnasium, say forty-nine of them were authentic eighteenth century cabinets, and one was handmade in the modern times. In five minutes, you could figure out which was the shill. How you ask? The fake would sit square because the structure would not be worn out by time. Moreover, the patina, which is that thin surface of the wood, would be thin on the recent one, and deep and well blended on the older ones. There is advanced technology to verify that, but it is expensive and not that accurate. You cannot duplicate the color that forms on wood through oxidation and ultra violent light over time. It's like vintage wine without the label. You might mistake it for vinegar, but you will always know it is old. No Hasseler will not add much to what I see."

"Of course, a clever person could forge all that," said Susan.

"Not really," said Harper raising his fork with his right hand. "Look at the boards on the back. They are so old they are almost near to rotten. I mean the core is solid, but that surface wood is soft and dried. Those board, I can tell you,-- those are typical eighteenth century boards. Yes, indeed, it's just something you learn over years by studying these things. The face boards on the front have a coating, probably some mixture of linseed oil, turpentine, and mineral spirits, plus many coats of wax, of course. Owners always waxed these things. Over the years, ultra violent light alters the substrata producing that patina and enriching the iridescence in a manner that no modern applied finish can duplicate. It's just aged wood."

Susan and Paul looked at each other with frozen stares. These very boards on the back were replaced by Crandall, who simply looked down at his plate while the older man went on.

The man rambled on, "As for, forgeries, there is the famous case of a Windsor Chair which was bought by experts at the Dearborn Museum by Henry Ford and his friends. It sat there in the museum for one year, as I recall. They believed it was made around 1700. Then one day, the creator, feeling guilty, announced that he forged it with hand tools from wood that he left out in the rain and cold just to age it. When Ford found it was a hoax, he loved the piece even more. As far as I know, it's still on display at Dearborn? A good forgery is a work of art in itself. But that does not apply to this piece."

Everyone enjoyed a good laugh at that story, and then Crandall looked quietly at Susan. He asked her once more. "So Susan, what do you think this Hasseler is going to say?" His voice had a nervous tone as if he wanted to change the subject.. "What's the mystery here? Is there some secret drawer that we have not found? Could there be a document in this drawer?"

Susan opened up and provided a detail she had not yet shared. "The previous owner remembered something about a group of people who either helped build something like this or hired someone else to build it. All he said was that he thought it was made in Lake County by the Mormon community, as it stood at that time, and that his father was there when this happened. Curiously enough, as far as I know, Hasseler has never seen the cabinet. I spent a good deal of time trying to describe this to him on the telephone. He said he might be wrong, but he insisted that he had to see it. And then he said, well, he said if this is the one he is looking for, there was actually something miraculous about how and why it was made."

"Miraculous?" said Crandall with a smile "Now we are taking this to another level!"

"Hey, that's my wife! Full of surprises," said Paul as he shook his head carefully, and looked with affection at her. She was a little put off by the cynical undertone of this all male conversation.

"I do not know what he meant, but that's what he said. Miraculous! But I do not want anyone, including my sarcastic husband to make fun of this man when he arrives here!"

"I'm sorry! I'm sorry!" said Paul who refrained from any form of laughter. "It's a miracle that it does not fall apart! Miracle that some one did not burn it up years ago. Ha! Ha! Miracles happen every day!"

"That's enough! Control yourself or leave."

"I'll be good," said Paul. "I'll behave. My point is we have to get the facts in order before we can move forward with this appraisal. And, we have a long way to go yet. Right? Is that fair?"

Crandall found this amusing. "No, the way I see it, this is a process of elimination. When all speculation has been removed, the thing will speak for itself. Now I really want to see this Hasseler, just so we can demonstrate the falseness of his claim. If, as you say, his father helped to build it, well that would place the date at around 1900. Were there still Mormons here in 1900? I don't know. That fellow who brought this up said the Mormons left around 1840. "

"I don't know," said Paul.

"Search me!" said Mr Harper. "Of course, we all want to see this Hasseler. But if he has never seen the cabinet, he is most likely thinking of something that has nothing to do with this piece. I have little doubt that what we have here is a case of mistaken identity. I'm sure when he sees it he will not recognize it at all. It is my belief that this piece was moved here from New England a century ago when it was already an antique. In the absence of any proof of this, we must take other opinions very seriously! There is after all a lot of money involved."

"Thank you all, including my husband!" said Susan. "As for another secret drawer, that's a possibility, but Mr. Hasseler has not shared anything like that with me. We do know of one secret drawer, right Crandall?"

"Yes, I'm going to address that drawer this afternoon. It's a very conventional drawer, but it adds some charm to the piece."

"Hasseler seems to be looking for something else," said Susan.

"Really?" said Crandall. "Well, you see, that complicates everything."

"Definitely," Harper said. "We have to talk to this man."

"Then, we have the issue of time. This is extremely important," said Crandall.

"How's that?" Paul asked as he leaned forward intent on hearing every word..

Crandall went on with this point. "One man, working alone, might spend years, I mean years, making this. This kind of man, the perfectionist and hobbyist woodworker, is very rare. A good co-operative shop with say eight men could do this in thirty days. But the lone man guided by passionate intensity takes forever. Time means nothing to him. The co-operative was common in the eighteenth century, but only a handful of cooperatives exist anymore. Now if Hasseler provides either evidence of a cooperative woodworking shop working around 1900, or some sort of extremely motivated, some spiritually motivated woodworker, that could be of interest to me. Chances are, he knows nothing of either. But that's not what he seems to be saying."

"I see what you mean," said Paul, "I saw a documentary once. It was about this monk in the Alps who carved statuary in hard wood. Each Madonna required five years of devotion to detailed carving by hand in the hardest wood. The monk never made a dime and never wanted to. He was grieving for his sins, grieving as I recall over a lost lover."

"Exactly! The tears of atonement! The passionate man who guides each incision of the chisel with an extreme skill, such men produced, not antiques, but art work," said Crandall. "That sort of craftsman complicates everything. Susan, your face just dropped. Is there something you want to share?"

She paused and smiled quietly. "This is all starting to make sense, but everything now hangs by a single thread."

"Harper, what's your input?" said Crandall.

"I believe most all the great art of the Renaissance, even of all history, was made this way. Maybe that's what we are looking at here. In such a case, we need to protect it. The value of such a work is difficult to establish. But once again, where's Hasseler?"

"Susan?" said Crandall. "You face seems puzzled. What are your thoughts on this?"

"The Intent," she said softly. "The intent of a soul? What was that woman trying to say?"

"Well," said Crandall. "Understanding the intent of another soul is the difference between the unknown and the unknowable. This is an area where persons of common sense draw a line. We must avoid speculation over the unknowable, tempting as it may be. We must stick with the facts."

"Yes, going beyond facts is not acceptable," said Mr. Harper. "Why are

we here? What is the meaning of life? That sort of thing. We don't have...
AH!.....we don't have a clue to the answers to such questions."

Paul drew a blank stare as he looked at everyone, concerned for a moment over his wife's sanity, and confused by his own lack of vocabulary. Confused about the money spent on artifacts.

"Hum," said Susan. "Somehow, I believe we may find out what the phrase 'intent of the soul' might mean today. You can see it carved into the detail by a devoted craftsman, but why did someone do that? What does it mean? What was the intent?"

Everyone laughed. They talked a few minutes on this matter before they dispersed. When they were to meet again in the main dining room, Crandall promised to talk to the entire group about the matter of the secret drawer. He said he would even show members of the group how to probe for a drawer with special instruments. This delighted Paul who loved the tangible feeling of tools.

Chapter Six

The Promising Peacocks

🏺

June 5, 1909

It was only a year after they moved into the country that Ebb and Jenny's destiny took a perilous turn. It began when the peacocks came, and that peculiar straw on the proverbial camel's back was enough to thrust them unto the mercy of a community they did not quite understand. It all began one afternoon at Ware's Castle when those glorious birds first arrived.

"Indeed, my dear, these peacocks are the most impertinent fowl!" said Mrs. Ware. She was a slightly plump middle-aged woman, with each gray hair perfectly set and curled. She maneuvered around in the yard in high black leather boots carefully manipulating a long stick with which she delicately prodded her two peacocks. Her teenage daughters laughed and teased each other as they threw breadcrumbs on the grass. Behind them was a curious house that some called Ware's Castle. It was a small blue stone cottage with a three story high turret, and an arched gateway that went through the west wing. This house was to serve as a gatehouse for the large sprawling mansion that was yet to be built somewhere high up in the woods.

A clear blue summer sky filled with promise embraced the most fortunate family as they ran about the lawn. The birds sometimes spread their wide tails as they jumped about nervously. Unable to fly at great lengths, they could leap over low objects and run at a good pace for a short distance. Neither of the girls were particularly attractive, yet they both had delicate manners and active imaginations. Julie, the older girl, had a chin so sloped back into her neck that from the side, she somewhat resembled a walrus. Nevertheless, she had a brilliant memory and could chant many

French and German poems as well as recite from memory about ten of Shakespeare's best sonnets, the rest she said were pure dribble. While Lydia, a gangling, active girl, with an arched nose, nevertheless had mastered the intricacies of both the violin and harp. Her music and her smile could soften the heart of all her gentlemen admirers. Neither of the girls worked a day in their lives, nor would they ever have to be concerned about money. Both continually complained about bugs and spiders and strange noises in the night. Obviously, more delicate than even the peacocks, they were not cut out for the rigors of a farm.

They were trying to guide the peacocks, named Henry and James, back behind their stone cottage built in the manor of a medieval castle. But the birds roamed over the three acre field in front of the house as if in search of a route back to paradise. Feargus down field dressed in his jodhpurs and hunting boots walked the perimeter. He herded the birds by waving a butterfly hoop over his head. "Get back there Super chicken! Go on up the slope super chicken," he hollered and laughed.

"Now dear, be gentle. We do not want to instill a fear of humans in our two friends. And you girls please, do not make so much commotion with all that laughter! Goodness!"

Up at the house, Ebb was thoroughly distracted by the whole scene and could scarcely keep his mind on his work. The small hunting lodge was more castle than house. It was over three stories high if you included the tall turret which served no recognizable purpose. In the east wing, there was the library where Feargus had his hunting trophies mounted amid favorite books of philosophy and literature. Ebb sawed and planed oak boards for a new book case. As he walked in and out of the library, he jerked around when the big birds occasionally squawked with the hideous sound of a banshee.

"Girls! Girls! Drive them back behind the house, but do it gently," said Feargus. In a few moments, they had the birds corralled behind the house, and the man who changed the oil business forever, came up to where Ebb worked humbly at his trade. They shared some small talk about the project, and then Feargus opened his soul for a rare moment that Ebb would never forget. "I think I have figured this thing out," he said.

"What's that you figured out?"

"Well, you know its pretty obvious, my two daughters are a mixed blessing. Oh I love them and the wife, but they sure do not hanker after this country life. They would much rather be back in a big city in a ballroom. That's why I brought those birds here. Gives them something to do. Not that there isn't plenty to do already, but they are not interested in hunting or farming, not the way boys might take up an interest in such things. You see, I like to keep them here as much as possible, but then they miss their social friends in Cleveland. So when I go away as I do frequently to Pittsburgh or Chicago on business, I get into trouble with the wife. That's one reason I like having you near here, you and that boy of yours can help keep an eye on things. You see, Ebb, when I'm not here, the misses gets agitated with the whole place. She just wants to sell it and move back to the city."

"I understand. My wife's the same way. I mean Jenny can hold her own for a while, but up there in the house on the hill, she sometimes sinks into a pit of despair."

"Most women are that way, but look at that bunch, fussing with those birds! This kind of pointless amusement makes them happy as singing larks at day break!" As he talked, Feargus walked up and down in the open entrance way between two sections of his high stone house. "How about you? Are you settling down, making any friends?"

"Well, oddly enough, the only friends I have are a bunch called the Mormons. They come through my place often. There's old lady Hasseler and her son, Billy, and then a fellow called Elmer Rodell with his wife and four kids. Those boys and mine go to school together."

"The Mormons. Yeah, I know them. Interesting folks. Although nothing that they say and write makes sense, everything that they do has an eternal meaning. Did you know this? They are direct descendants from those Pilgrim folks who first came here from England in 1640's. That's a fact. They know how to take care of their own. There was a lot more of them here sixty years ago, but things got mixed up and they headed out west. Some even were killed by vigilantes. These are remarkably stubborn people. Persistent in what they believe and do."

"You don't say. Are they Christians or what?"

"Well Ebb, I'm no authority on that, so don't take my word on it for true. But as I understand it, Joseph Smith, their founding prophet, found some gold plates up on a hill in New York. He took those plates and translated them into English, and as it turns out, they pretty much retold the same moral story as we find in the Bible only it's about the Indians here in America."

"You don't say!"

"Yes, that's a fact. They claim in their Bible that some tribes of the Ancient Hebrews came across the ocean a long, long time ago, and they became the Indians. Those tribes did quite well for a while. They built mounds, had fine cities and even roads, and had a pretty fine civilization. Then things fell apart. A new generation went wild, broke away from the old order, and then plundered the wiser people. The Indians we see or hear about are wild remnants of some vaster civilization."

"That's something I often wondered about myself," said Ebb.

"So, these folks, these Mormons, they take all this with the deepest seriousness. They stick together. They help each other, and they will pray for everyone because they believe this world will not last much longer. Jesus is coming back soon and things are going to change like you never would believe. Now, I'm startin' to sound like a preacher!"

"Well that's believable enough! This world's in a bad way. Folks in the cities have lost their skills in survival. And as for modern inventions, why they've created more problems than they've solved."

"The Mormons don't drink, don't cuss, don't fight unless they have to to survive, and more than any people I know, they take care of their own. They live like one big family. Actually, they appear to be descendants of the Anglo Saxon tribes that lived in England, a long, long time ago, a tough and timeless people, but loving and charitable."

"You know, I noticed what you're saying is true. They're always after us to join up with them."

Feargus smiled and shook his head, "They do that to everyone."

"Well, they can't be all bad as some say."

"Well, some church folks, like the Baptist, don't like that Bible of theirs. But you know, they read the Holy Scriptures just like everyone else. The Mormons were schooled in the tough school of the American frontier. Those times were tough, but those folks endured by sticking up for each other, no matter what happened. That temple up there on the hill, they built that tall building themselves by sacrificing everything they had. Then, they fell on hard times, and had to leave it behind and march out West. That took a lot of faith and courage. You have to respect them for that Joseph Smith, their leader, he was martyred out there in Carthage. That instilled even more determination in them. Most of them moved on to the mountains and deserts in Utah." Feargus looked around the back of the stone house to where the girls penned in the peacocks. He said, "Well, here I am talking to you when I have plenty to do. I told the boys over at the stable to hitch a wagon so I can run into Willowford and pick up some things. While you are working here, just keep an eye on those birds. They are not quite use to my daughters and this place either."

He took off walking across the field toward the stables at a brisk pace. While Ebb worked on his shelving project, he thought to himself about the Mormons when he suddenly remembered how he spooked Elmer more than once by claiming he was an Erie Indian. He decided he ought to be more careful how he said that since Elmer probably took it to heart and prayed day and night for Ebb's lost soul. He laughed at that thought. "I'm an Erie Indian, and I hunt with my bare hands and a big stone knife! So don't mess with me," he thought to himself. He not only said that more than once, but taught his son to behave in such an outlandish manner. He amused himself thinking about that all day.

Scarcely a week passed after that conversation when tragedy reared its ugly face. It happened one Tuesday morning. Ebb asked Donny to come down to the blue stone Gatehouse with him and spend the day working instead of fishing. At breakfast, the two of them talked about the peacocks. They could not help laughing.

Ebb said, "Could you image those girls chasing those peacocks around the yard, and Mrs. Ware swinging this long pole, and Feargus yelling and swinging the butterfly hoop. It was the funniest thing!"

"Folks say she's not goin to last out here in the country. I mean she's from England, and has a big house in Cleveland. That castle they built next to the woods is in a pretty wild place," Jenny talked nervously as she fried some bacon and eggs on the cast iron wood burning stove.

"She's does fine, but those birds make me nervous."

"What's a peacock do anyway?" Donny asked.

"They strut around like a preacher and fan their big tails!" Ebb made weird gestures with his chest and arms while he talked about the birds.

'They put those feathers in big hats, I think!" Jenny said.

"Not in my hat!" Ebb said and winked at his son.

"I'm talkin' bout the refined hats of proud ladies."

"I know, and yet in spite of their beauty, they leave the same mess on the grass just like geese and ducks."

"Now that's enough of that," she said.

"What do they eat?" the boy asked.

"Grain and oh yeah, dried old bread. Here son take some of these old biscuits with you just in case we get a chance to feed the rascals."

Soon they were out the door where Ebb had the horse, Finny, already hitched to a wagon, and they started along the road that led to Ware's Castle, as some folks called it.

"I can't wait to see the peacocks. Are they bigger than turkeys?"

"About shoulder high to you if you stood up on your toes. Don't get too near 'em they might peck your eye out and eat it," he said.

"Nah!"

"Sure enough, they can be mean as the devil!"

It took about twenty minutes to get to the house. Shortly after arriving, they parked the wagon and carried some wood and tools up to the gatehouse to work. Lydia and Julia came carrying a small basket of grain for the peacocks. "Good morning, Mr. Collard and Donny," Julia, the poetess, hollered out as she skipped along the gravel path behind the house. "I see you brought your son. Do you think he would like to help us feed Henry and James?"

"Well, Donny never seen a peacock before!"

"Oh then come along with us. We're going right now!"

It was most unusual for these two girls to be out so early doing chores. But the peacocks were special. Ebb and Donny dropped everything and followed them up the path to the pen near edge of the deep woods. It was a beautiful morning. The huge oak and tulip trees towered like giant gods all the way up the steep hill behind the house. The green and eager leaves fluttered as if eager to greet the rising sun. Hundred of birds sang hidden high up in the branches. A gentle brook, fed by a local spring, splashed over the flat rocks and spilled over the edge of a stone dam before whirling around in a playful run on its way to the Chagrin.

They had not walked fifteen steps where Lydia holler out in a loud voice. "Oh No! No!" Then she dropped to her knees, and fainted right on the trail. Julie dropped her basket and turned and ran back toward the house screaming. Ebb and Donny ran forward to see what happened. There they were. James limped around with one broken leg. Henry with his left wing twisted backward. Donny stepped through a hole in the fence where the screening had been ripped apart by some strong animal. He saw where the grain pan and the water bucket had been tipped over during a violent attack. He reached down and picked up one tail feather that probably could still adorn a refined woman's hat. "Is this one of those feathers, you were talkin about pop? " he asked. But the rare birds were wounded now, still alive but badly crippled and in need of serious care.

Ebb did not hear Donny's question because, filled with fear, he had already reached down and picked up Lydia in his arms and carefully carried her back toward the house.

"What happened? " Donny hollered as he followed them.

"Looks like a bobcat, maybe a wolf came down and attacked them birds. Must have been during the night."

"No, pop, I see it here. It was only a big old raccoon. But he's dead. The birds pretty well ripped him apart."

He could hear Julia hollering up by the house, "Father! Father! Some animal attacked Henry and James!"

Feargus came running barefoot with only his trousers and his undershirt on. "Something wrong with my baby! What happened to my baby?" he said.

"I believe she fainted. Looks like a raccoon got into the pen and attacked the peacocks. Made a mess of the place. The birds are still alive though. They got the best of the fight. Raccoon's dead."

"Bring her on up and put her on the couch! You know, I was trying to make it pleasant back here for ladies, that's all. I was trying to make life pleasant!" Feargus' voice cracked, as the man fought back tears. Ebb never believed that staunch man could be brought so low. It reminded him of many faces at the Great Fire.

They all went up into the stone cottage where Ebb carried the girl inside and placed her gently on the couch by a window so she could catch air. Feargus searched wildly through a cabinet for a touch of smelling salts. Donny glanced all around the room and tried to get a glimpse of the girl's pale face. He had never been in the castle before. After a quick snort, the girl woke up and cried and cried as Mrs. Ware comforted her.

After things settled down a bit, Mrs. Ware looked across the room at Feargus who leaned on the back of a chair, shaking his head. "This is it!" she said in a firm voice. "I'm done with this place. No more castles. No more temples. No more farming and hunting! No more wild animals attacking our gentle pets. This is it! I told you before, and now I'm telling you again! I'll have no more of this wilderness!! We are going back to the city as soon as possible. And we will remain there!"

"I know!" said Feargus as he saw his vision of the sprawling English countryside perish into ashes right before his eyes.

"Well mam, you don't have to worry none," said Donny, interrupting the ongoing family quarrel. "Those peacocks ripped that coon apart! Those birds shredded 'em good! They took a beating though. It musta been some fight!"

"Thank you, Master Donald, for that precious piece of cherished information," said Mrs. Ware, as her blank face trembled while she studied her husband, waiting for one wise crack.

"Your welcome, mam. May I make one special request, mam?"

"What might that be?" she said staring at her husband, waiting for the amused grin.

"Could I have the pelt?"

"The pelt?" she said looking at her husband, who stood stark silent trying to conceal a smile.

"Yeah, that's the coon's fir. Makes a fine hat, seein' as it came from a special fight."

"Indeed, it did. Consult with Mr. Ware on that important matter," she said stoned faced and determined as she stared down her husband. "Any other requests?"

"No, Mam. That's about it."

"Oh, God," said Julia, the Shakespearean poetess, as she fell back in a chair and looked up at the ceiling.

In a few minutes, Lydia sat up and looked around as if she did not know where she was, "Oh, mother, some terrible beast assaulted Henry and James! I thought I heard them squawking last night! I should have ran back there. I feel so bad. I failed them!" Tears poured down her face.

Ebb looked at Donny's blank face and then the broken face of Feargus and his wife. It was like Elmer had said. These gentle folks did not belong in this rugged wilderness. He felt as if his whole life was suspended by a frail thread and that thread now unraveled right before his eyes. His land, his job, his family's security depended on this place and those visionary plans that Feargus had shared with him, and for which, Feargus alone brought all of them out here to live like gentle farmers endowed with immense wealth.

Ebb knew right then this way of life was over.

Chapter Seven

Fishing on The Chagrin

As expected, given the nature of the man, Feargus departed from the Chagrin Valley with the same expedience as when he arrived ten years earlier. The man moved on to better things even if they were worse; it was just part of his nature to be positive no matter what happened. But as a token of thanks, he left his beloved handy man with an interesting opportunity.

Only a month after Feargus vacated the castle, he sent Ebb a real estate contract allowing him to buy the ten acres, with the farmhouse, the barn, the stable, and the hand dug cistern for a mere $2,400, in payments of $21.33 for eight years with credit for previous rent paid. Ebb did not try to figure it out, he took the contract to a notary, had it registered in the County Court House, and dispatched a copy back to Feargus. He now held a mortgage on the farm.

Some months later, a new resident arrived in the stone Gatehouse, but he did not plan to hire Ebb in any capacity, so Ebb drove around the country in his wagon looking for any kind of work he could find. He found odd jobs here and there, but nothing like the security he once enjoyed. Between jobs, he dedicated an excess of his free time to the supremely important task of teaching the young boys the lore of fishing and hunting. Building a grand secretary desk in his stable was now the least of his concerns. It was all but forgotten. Life had gotten in the way.

A year earlier, the trio of young boys, Billy Hasseler, Chris and Steve Rodell cut their own trail through the woods as they explored a secret route up a narrow stream to the hill to where the loner Donny lived with his reclusive parents. All four boys were at that irresponsible age when wrestling and tree climbing and racing through the deep forest at mid night evoked powerful and magical feelings. Those boys lived in defiance of civilization. The adult world, with its capricious rules contrived to subdue the natural spirit, did not interest them in the least. While Jenny weeded her tomatoes and beans and fussed over her chickens, and Ebb worked at odd jobs, Donny pretty much found ways for more important things like swinging on grape vines over deep ravines and leaping over steep embankments without so much as twisting his ankle. His three friends, though less inclined to rowdiness because they were schooled in the solemn manners of the Mormons, secretly emulated Donny when no adults were around to take a switch to them.

There were, of course, crimes of a petty sort. These included stealing grapes from vineyards, apples and peaches from orchards, and nighttime raids on empty barns where the most daring leaped from dangerous, high beams into deep mounds of hay. Often, on the next day, some farmer would spend all morning trying to remember where he left a handy pocket knife needed to cut twine. Although such knives usually ended up in a metal box hidden in a small crevice in Ebb's barn, no one knew how or why this collection grew at such an alarming rate. It must have been Indians that put them there, or maybe a woodland ghost, certainly no kids owned knives like that.

It was late in the spring of 1910 that Ebb found time to take the whole crew down the Chagrin River in canoes. It was something he had no time for, but he did it anyway. The quietude of the river often allows dark thoughts to surface among those who harbor restless memories. Ebb had to fish, seeing as he grew up on a farm, but when he turned twenty and began his family life, he became a city man. But his memories of the city were dark, traumatized, foreboding. Thus this venture began with the sound of small stones hitting the upper window on Hasseler farm house at about five in the morning, but it would not remain that gentle. The trauma was always there.

One stone followed another, until Billy's blond head and half opened eyes appeared behind the glass. "Hey wild Bill, let's go!" Donny whispered from the yard below.

"I'll be right down," the boy whispered back to him from a half open window

Ebb held the reins in his hands as he sat in the wagon out by the Chillicothe Road and waited . He thought of his own wild youth and wondered where he had lost that happy innocence. Finny snorted and impatiently stomped his hoof on the dirt road. It was about a year since the peacock fiasco, and by this time Ebb had become a garrulous sage to the neighborhood kids. Although the money was short, the more important matter of river fishing had its own rewards. Ebb sat there with Finny, looking at the sunrise, the clouded sky over head, and his pocket watch. Even a slight tardiness agitated his restless soul. He looked back at the house for some activity. "Where are those darn boys," he mumbled.

In matter of moments, both boys came running, leaped up on the sides of the wagon, and sat down atop the tarps and the sleeping bags and back packs, carefully not putting even the slightest pressure on the long thin poles and the carefully crafted lures.

"You didn't wake your mom did you son?" Ebb asked as he snapped the reins.

"Only for a moment."

"She's knows you will be gone over night, now?"

"Oh, yeah, I explained the plan last night."

"Okay. Cause if she knows where you're going and how long, and if you bring back a fair catch, well, then you've done all you can do to please her, and by golly, you might just earn a license to fish again. Get a woman riled about it, and you'll never hear the end of it." Ebb snapped the reins as the horse moved along the trail.

The boys looked at each other and laughed. "She's fine. Which way we headed?" Billy asked as he scratched the thick blond hair that sat on his head like an inverted bird's nest. He rubbed the sand out of his pale blue eyes.

"Down to the wooden bridge above Steele's Mill," Ebb said as he prodded the horse. "Elmer and his two boys should be there now with three wooden canoes . We will have two guys in each canoe. Chagrin should be running smooth after that rain yesterday." Few words were spoken as they followed the trail. Down in the river valley, they passed by a wall of heavy rock that had been pushed over thousands of years ago, when the last great glacier called the Wisconsin Ice Sheet, came down from the North pole and reshaped the landscape leaving behind steep beautiful valleys; the Lake Erie basin itself was a product of that same massive ice sheet. In fact , ice from the glacier made the entire system called the Great Lakes, the largest body of fresh water on the planet and left behind some great fishing holes which they were about to raid.

It was a quiet and cool morning, wherein a few birds had just begun to sing in the tall trees. High up in a red oak tree, Donny spotted a tall pileated woodpecker, with a big red plum and body nearly a foot long. From on high, it appeared to follow the wagon as it descended into the valley.

In those days, and especially on that early morning, it seemed as if nothing of earth shaking importance had happened for thousands of years in that secluded woodland valley. As far as it was known, a primitive people, the Erie were the first humans to explore the area. When they vanished, they left behind only scattered traces of their primitive hunting grounds. These were spindle stones, about the size of footballs, each stone had a small one inch hole drilled into the center. They could still be found in large piles heaped up on the tops of hills. These stones were tools for grinding grains and herbs. Then there were arrowheads and spearheads; usually such things turned up when a field was plowed. Their frailty reminded the finder of how difficult it must have been to survive in those ancient times. And then there were the trails themselves. They usually followed along the ridges to some point where they descended into the valleys. Some of these old trails remained in the form of the narrow winding roads, such as the one they followed on that morning.

"One time," said Ebb, "up on those hills to the Southeast, when I was a kid, I came here with some hunters, and we found a huge black rock, with a face crudely carved in it. That face looked like the cross behind a human and cat's face. It was about the size of child's face and had eye sockets about the size of a half dollar. It is probably still up there somewhere. A most serious face, I have never seen another carved like that."

"Who do you think carved it pa?"

"An Indian, probably an Erie Indian. Must have taken a long time too."

"Why?" said the other boy.

"Why what?" said Ebb.

"Why did he carve it?"

"To remember....to remember something terribly sad, I reckon. It just looked that way to me. I say this remembering the eyes on that face. Something very sad happened up there, a long time ago, way beyond the memory of anyone living." The secluded hills, the relaxed moment, all conjured the spirit of another place somewhat beyond time. Ebb encouraged that kind of thinking on these fishing trips because he believed it opened up some portal of harmony and balance, a sixth sense which monitored all reckless behavior and focused everyone on survival. It was necessary to think like that when you grew up in the wilds. But at the same time, it conjured up memories he did not want to share, memories he wanted to bury as deep as he could, memories that persisted like flashes of lightning.

When they reached the bridge, they met Elmer and his two sons. They had already arranged the three canoes so that they were halfway out of the river which ran swiftly since yesterdays rain. The gear of tents and food was carefully dispersed in the canoes with room for more. Elmer spoke with generous laughter and a big smile as he brought out a rough sketch of a map that he had made on previous trips. He pointed out some possible fishing holes and landmarks that he expected to see along the way. He showed where they would camp for the night before they moved on to where the river emptied out into Lake Erie. Above the Lake on the mouth of the river, they would camp one last night, if the weather permitted.

While the men were busy with the map, the boys hauled their gear out of the wagon and secured it in the canoes. Suddenly Ebb heard an unusual popping and humming sound. He looked up the Mill Road where a dark buggy with rubber tires and no horse came quickly. This machine pulled up on the field and stopped near the men and the wagon. "Where on earth did you get that? " said Ebb and scratched his head.

"Why that's a Model T Ford!" said Elmer. "Do you mean to tell me you never seen one before?"

"Well, now I've seen some horseless carriages in the city, but they were mostly big and fancy machines that always broke down. This little devil is like a little buggy." The men walked around as they examined the dark black machine with its hooped fenders that hovered over the red spoked wheels. Under the hood, Ebb discovered a gasoline engine not much bigger than a sewing machine. It hummed in a low rhythm resemblance of a pump. "Hop on board and take a ride," said Elmer. "This here's Brother Abner Steele and Brother Morley. They are my friends from the Church. They will take your horse and wagon back up to your barn soon after we embark. Hey, we have a few minutes! Give all these fellows a ride around the pasture."

"Hello, gentlemen, we've met on a few occasions around town." said Ebb as he climbed up front. Donny hopped in the back as Abner revved up the engine, put her in gear, and drove around the field in figures eights while the other boys ran around behind waving branches as if they were in a parade.

"I thought only the rich folks had machines like this!" Ebb shouted.

"Not since Ford came along and brought the price down to where the average fellow can get one!" Abner laughed and talked. This man would play a very serious role in his life. As for now, he spun the car around and around until a rear wheel inevitably dropped into a drainage ditch and started to spin in the mud. Then everyone but Abner hopped out and putting their shoulders to the bumper and fenders, they boosted her out of the ditch, and she took off running like a squirrel

Ebb walked back to where Elmer stood. He spat on the ground and said, "New fangled world we live in."

"You could get one of those. Of course, they're just about worthless in winter. You'll always need a horse. No way around that. But that little bugger is faster and easier to run than any horse," Elmer said.

"Useless in winter, you say!"

"Sure enough."

Ebb looked across the field at that funny looking car as it spun around on the grass. Those words brought a smile to his face. "Useless when you need it the most!" he mumbled.

There were no white caps or rushing surges on the gentle Chagrin. Just swift currents running steady like time does when you step back for a moment and watch the clouds and breeze in the trees. The restless movements of the natural world never ceased; seemed to continue without either a start or a finish He was anxious now to set out and follow those currents down stream as far as confluence of the east and west branches where they would camp late in the afternoon. It reminded him of freedom. "This coming winter, I hope to begin making my big cabinet back in the stable. Show it to you sometime. After the snow falls, won't be much else to do," he said as he loaded the canoe.

"Sure! I've heard about that project somewhat. Feargus once told me it was a right fascinating little cabinet. I'd like to see it some day. Come on Chris!" Elmer yelled at the top of his voice, "Bring that gang over here! We're settin' out right now! No more delays!" He stepped into the canoe and climbed toward the bow, carefully keeping it from flipping by balancing himself with a paddle..

Soon six figures in three canoes navigated the flowing stream easing their way amid the jutting rocks. Strung out in a line about ten foot apart, the voyagers looked up with awe at the lush green trees and the steep cliffs built on layer upon layer of thin , gray shale; and beyond the tree line, nothing but blue sky.

Chapter Eight

The Secret Drawer

It was almost three o'clock when Crandall summoned the group together for his lecture on the secret drawer. Of course, by this time, some disgruntled visitors had departed and a few late comers had arrived, but there remained more than a modicum of curiosity about the old secretary which did not move from its skewed position by the door. There was an unwritten consensus, derived from spurious gossip, that those rough cut boards on the back insured the cabinet as an eighteenth century masterpiece. This was precisely what Crandall wanted to hear. But still, he felt a need to firm up his presentation just in case this Hasseler showed up with some spurious information.

Just before he began speaking, Susan went out the front door to the stately porch. She made a critical cell phone call to the airport. While she walked back and forth with restless determination, Crandall maintained his poise as he pursed his lemon shaped face in a pontifical manner, and defended his date.

"We know that in the Eighteenth Century both political and military organizations could not be trusted anymore than we can trust these institutions in our time. We know today that privacy is a major issue for our survival. Big Brother, the proverbial spy behind the camera, is everywhere. Well, it is therefore no surprise that the Secretary Desk became a keeper of deep, sometimes personal secrets, that is, of course, the origin of the word secretary, designating a keeper of secrets.

"Most secretaries had at least one or two secret drawers where confidential information such as, perhaps a deed to property, perhaps a hand written will, even perhaps cash or other negotiable instruments were tucked away. When we open a secretary, we meet a series of drawers and pigeon holes, as you see here." He pulled down the lid to its flat position and revealed about twenty small drawers, each neatly carved. He pulled out one delicate drawer and held it up to his audience. "This area is sometimes referred to as the gallery, and this object is clearly a visible drawer. No secrets about that.

"Now, this drawer as you can see by this ruler is seven inches in length. When I place this ruler here below the gallery and measure the depth we can see it is seven inches deep. Many secret drawers consist of nothing more than a small box behind the regular drawers. So that if this was six inches in length and the depth of the gallery was seven inches, then with a little probing with a flash light and a hooked device like this clothes hanger wire, we often discover a hidden drawer behind any one of these or even all of them. That is perhaps the most common sort. Now, let us examine this drawer. Yes, a five inch drawer in a seven inch slot. Now carefully, reaching back in there, I insert my wire in a small hole and here it is! As you can see, a small two inch box, probably a safe place for jewelry.

"Another type of drawer can found behind a brace or column which appears at first glance to be a solid stabilizing pillar. But when we pull the edge of the pillar loose, we discover that the whole thing is a hollow box or secret drawer. I have photographs of both of these types which I will pass around. Another type often found is a hollow box fitted into one of the major boards that supports the lid. Then there are some that hide behind sliding panels in the sides. Another frequent type is found above or below these four main drawers in the front." Crandall went on talking for fifteen minutes while he handed out photographs of all sorts of drawers found in famous cabinets. When he was done, he asked for questions.

"Well, I feel I have to ask this," said a young woman in the front. "Do you ever find anything, say love letters in these drawers? I saw a movie about that once."

"Usually not. The owners clear these things out before they turn them over to museums. But it may surprise you to learn that, there are cases, rare indeed, when secretaries and cabinets have been on display in museums for years and suddenly, while moving or probing around, some one will find a secret drawer with a document such as a letter or some money in it."

"Well," said Bob Harper, the man with the big gold ring, "Could there still be another drawer in this one? I assume you have looked."

Crandall smiled in his usual condescending manner. "I have probed this cabinet from top to bottom. I have disassembled it in many places. I have used earphones and small wooden hammer to search for hollow places. To my knowledge, it has one secret drawer which is a small box behind this drawer on the left. That box is easily retrievable. Right here, and as you can see, this little box is empty. It could have once held a piece of fine jewelry. I mean it's large enough."

"I have a question," said Paul who had been sitting in the back halfway listening and halfway watching the nervous agitation of his wife as she paced up and down on the porch talking on her cell phone.

"Yes, Paul."

"I have never heard of this drawer until now. When did you find it?"

"When I took the cabinet to my shop for examination."

"When was that?" Paul asked.

"I would say three weeks ago. Yes, I thoroughly examined it for five days."

"When you found the drawer was there anyone else there with you?"

"No. I was alone. I mean I cannot afford a research assistant."

"And what was in the drawer?"

"Absolutely nothing."

"Not even some scrap of paper or a button or a postage stamp. Or something with a date."

"No, nothing at all. Why does this amuse you? Do you think I would conceal something that I found in the drawer?"

"Well, you know Crandall, I'm not Sherlock Holmes or nothing like that, but it just seems odd that you concealed the fact that there was a secret drawer. I mean if it was my cabinet, which in a way it is, that's the first thing I would be telling people. Maybe its just me."

"Well, it's a common thing to find a secret drawer with no secret in it."

"But that's not my point," said Paul. "This Colladaire guy, this guy who built this same kind of cabinet, I mean did he put the same kind of drawer in similar places on his other cabinets. I guess that's what I 'm getting at.

Was this his style so speak? Can we link the cabinets by the drawers? Do you get what I'm trying to say?"

Crandall folded his arms across his stomach in a gesture of defense. He was slightly embarrassed by this question. "The secret drawer would be placed where the owner wanted it, which was not always the same as where the cabinet maker might want it to be. So this was not unusual. It was common to place a drawer where this one is."

"Yeah. Sort of like hiding a spare key under your car fender or your bumper," said Paul with a kind of circular rotation of his right hand.

"Same thing."

"And you don't think the way that's done is important."

"Well, it could be. But in this case, it's meaningless."

"Yeah. I see what you mean. Nothing is in the drawer. It's in a plain old place. So who cares? Well then could there be a real secret drawer somewhere else? Maybe this one was just a shill to make you think you had found the one and only secret drawer. You know, I've been thinkin' all along that maybe this Hasseler guy who is supposed to be here any time now. Maybe he knows where the real secret drawer is, and maybe he does not want us to know until he gets here. Maybe in that is the answer to who made this thing. You see, he wants to open it himself."

"Well," Crandall said as he lifted both his hands in acceptance of the point being made, "We will have to ask him that when he gets here, won't we?"

At the moment, Susan came in from porch with her lips buttoned up tight as if everything that could wrong did go wrong. Everyone turned toward her with a stone silent look. "Susan, you look a little pale," said Crandall. "Is something wrong?"

"No, but Mr Hasseler did not make his flight. I left a message on his answering machine. Right now, it seems no one knows where he is. So, let's have some dessert!"

The whole group began chattering with confusion, as they moved to another room still talking about Hasseler and the secret drawer. "Well, I hope he's all right," said one woman.

"I hope he exists," said Paul in a humorous tone.

Susan delivered a callous glance at her husband.

Chapter Nine

The Great Blue Heron

In the country, men and their sons must hunt, fish, and camp together. It is all part of a ritual of passage by which the generations bind themselves to the land. Without this ritual, the women, who frequently have trouble tolerating the antics of campers, will suffer more than the men. Through this ritual, the young lose their fear of the wilderness and in so doing become not just men, but warriors, that is, protectors of their families. It is an essential and sometimes fearful passage.

Into this ritual, Ebb brought his dark memory.

So it was, traumatic undertones streamed through his and his son's minds on the day they took that trip in three canoes downstream. The steady lull of the water rippled quickly and spryly around the jutting rocks. It was not white water in the torrential sense, for the Chagrin was a shallow flat stream, deep only at occasional whirling basins, and even then, only after a big storm. But the solemn mood extended into the tree tops where the signs of summer moved among green leaves as if some ghostly spirit swept through the branches. The mood gained intensity when Donny, the point man at the bow of the first canoe, spotted a Great Blue Heron.

Alarmed, this stately blue grayish bird with stilt legs and an s-curved neck, looked up and jerked its head as if to capture quick snapshots of the intruders. Donny signaled for everyone to be still and pull up their paddles. As they drifted, they silently watched the bird. It stood in mid stream, perched on the jutting corner of a flat rock. At first, it waited for them as they came around a sharp bend in the stream. Its solitude now broken, it ceased feeding and nurturing itself, as it jerked its head three or four different ways. As they approached, gracefully in a slow symphonic movement, it spread its wide wings and launched into a low flight over the river, suspended as it seemed by invisible threads descending from heaven. Then it landed, once more in mid stream, and jerked its head three or four different angles, and watched as the intruders slowly advanced.

Donny guided the point canoe to the left bank and beckoned for the others to follow, as he attempted to make a pass around the Blue Heron. But the great bird, as if now engaged in some sort of uncanny play, alighted again, rose about five feet above the water, and glided about thirty or forty feet, where it set down on another jutting rock. Its feet struggled for a moment before it found a way to grip the slippery rock, and it turned much as a trained dog might turn its head backwards to see if the intruders were still there. To the campers, it appeared to be leading them somewhere. This time Donny made a pass across the river which was about forty to fifty feet wide; he hoped to pass by the bird much closer. But to no avail, for just as soon as he came near the bird, the Blue Heron lifted its big wings and advanced further ahead.

At this point, the bird began to annoy Donny, so he guided his canoe back toward the center of the river, where a channel of water ran swiftly. Once in this channel, his canoe surged ahead, but the Blue Heron seemed amused by these antics; it lifted its wings once more and glided casually ahead always maintaining a safe distance of about fifty feet ahead of the canoe. This cat and mouse game continued for about fifteen minutes, until Donny became frustrated with the recurring pattern and slapped the water with his paddle. "Get out of the way!" he yelled. The sound of his voice resonated off the steep cliffs.

Suddenly the Blue Heron, alighted and flapped his wings in a powerful surge and rose to a higher level, perhaps thirty to forty feet over the River, and then it made a wide arcing U-turn with wings out stretched in a five foot span as it chose a safer route close to the tree line on the west side of the river. From high up, it drifted swiftly back up stream and returned most likely to the exact same place where it was first seen. After that, the canoes drifted aimlessly down river. The crew of six, entranced by the majesty of this noble creature, searched excitedly for another Blue Heron, but there was only one divine messenger, and there would be no other.

Ebb, who watched all this with amusement, knew why the Blue Heron left in haste. His son was not at ease with creation. Ebb knew why. He said nothing. He smiled to himself. It was the grievin'.

In those days, the river was still pristine. Fish, turtle, raccoon, and the playful, chattering birds thrived on the lush life and felt secure as they moved about freely in the deep solitude. The water was drinkable, the air untainted, and all sounds belonged to eternity. In this calm atmosphere, as if representatives of an ensuing calamity, the boys became restless. About one o'clock, after a half hour of tranquility, Donny stood up and said, "I want to take the rear for a while!" He shouted for Chris to move as he started clambering over the backpacks. The canoe rocked precariously from side to side. He tripped and fell over Chris. "Whoa there! I almost lost my balance!" he said as both began laughing.

"Quit pulling on my shirt!" Chris hollered, and with that, Chris stood up and the canoe made a sharp turn and flipped over in the shallow water perhaps no more than two feet deep. All of the luggage sank to the bottom as both boys fell over and rose up standing knee deep in the stream laughing hysterically.

"Foolishness! Damn foolishness!" said Ebb as he stalled his canoe with a paddle. He quickly jumped out into the stream and held the prow with a firm grip so his canoe would not flip. The third canoe, with the younger boys in command, turned toward the shallows at the shoreline, hit gravel, and stopped.

"That was totally unnecessary!" said Elmer as he jammed his paddle into a crevice and stepped out into the stream. "Now flip that over and pull all that gear out of the river before it soaks through and ruins everything. Move! Don't stand there gawkin' and laughin' like a couple of hyenas. You don't have time!"

But hyenas or not, the young boys could not stop laughing as they wrestled with the canoe and the baggage. Ebb waded carefully through the water with a dead eye bead on Donny and when he got near him, he reached over and flipped him backward and pushed his head below the surface. With an iron grip on his neck, he held his head there for a few seconds before he lifted him up. "So you want to be a fool, do you!" Ebb yelled. "People get hurt with that kind of foolishness." He flipped him back into water once more time and then walked away.

Donny rose quickly, shaking the water off his head.

"Baptized! You just been baptized! Now you are a real Mormon!" yelled Chris.

Everyone laughed, even Elmer who tried not to as he turned and shook his head.

Donny reached down into the stream and pulled up the dripping wet sleeping bag. He covered his face as he laughed in low, quiet undertones. A young hero, undaunted by the rough abuse of his father, he said nothing after that but kept a subdued grin, winking at the other boys as he reloaded the canoe.

"I'll teach that boy religion one way or another," said Ebb as he waded up stream to his canoe.

After about fifteen minutes, most all the gear in the river was recovered. Whatever was not, belonged to nature forever. They moved all the canoes to the shallows and climbed on board and maneuvered into the flowing current.

"Sorry, Elmer, but that kid of mine has no sense," Ebb said.

"He's a wild one, all right," Elmer said in a low tone. "Let it all go."

And they moved on.

By mid afternoon, they were at the confluence of the East and West Branches. They jumped out of the canoes and climbed up the gravel and mud bank where they secured the prows with ropes. Huge cottonwood trees hung their lazy limbs over the field and the river. In late May, these trees blossomed with soft flowers like snow that dropped a blanket of pollen over the entire valley. This pollen brought many folks to sneezing and tearing for a few weeks. But at this time, they had not yet broken out. All around the valley itself which extended for about twenty acres, there were high cliffs formed of loose shale, not good for climbing. These cliffs, which soared upward about five hundred feet, had been there since the last Glacier retreated ten thousand years ago. This was certainly a great hunting and fishing ground for the ancient Erie, who were once a proud and powerful people. Long ago, many tribes resided in the hills within about a thirty mile radius of this point.

"Boys," said Ebb, inspired by the scenery. "You can tell looking around that this had to be a main gathering point for the Erie. We'll camp here for the night. So let's remember our native friends who learned how to enjoy a good lunch in the wilderness!" With that, he opened a small sack, which contained smoked deer jerky, cheese, and homemade bread. He set the food on the grass atop a red neckerchief, which he used like a plate. He cut and ate his food with the same hunting knife he used to clean fish and cut rope, but he did remember to flush the blade clean with canteen water before he started slicing his food.

The boys followed in a similar manner, except for Donny and Chris who had to lay their gear out on the grass to let it dry. That took a while. They returned to snickering and calling each other foul names as they ate their water soaked bread.

"You know, Ebb," said Elmer as he ate his lunch, "Talk about history, it was just eighty years ago that the first Mormons lived in farmhouses, cabins, and primitive camps too, and that was just about a mile up that East Branch stream right over in the gorge. That's the way to Kirtland all right. I'll take you up there sometime. Also, not far from where we are, they baptized the new members right in the river. I'd like to show you the famous places there. Some very miraculous things happened up that way in the old days. And you know, talk about surviving in the wilderness, why there were upwards of three thousand of them living off the land, as I recall from stories I heard as a boy."

"Who brought them here?" said Ebb.

"The Prophet. He believed the world was coming into an new age and that he was gathering all the saints who believed in the restored gospel. Many fled from New York to avoid persecution for their faith."

"But they did not remain here, why's that?" said Ebb.

"The Lord had a new plan for them. They went all the way out to the Rocky Mountains, yes, sir, all the way to Utah to carry out their purpose."

"Why would anyone want to go that far?" Ebb asked.

"Because, they wanted to live in Zion, a place where everyone lived in a happy community with a pure heart! They sought to be an example to the whole world."

Ebb looked up and askance, and blurted out his own philosophy, " A pure heart, you say! A pure heart always suffers because of some darned community! I know that much! That's why I moved to the edge of the wilderness. To purify my own heart!"

Both men laughed. Elmer said, "Ebb, you have the strangest notions."

"Oh, you think so. I lived in Collin Wood just east of Cleveland for many years. Something that happened there burned a big hole right through my pure heart forever. But I don't want to talk about it here and now. In fact not anywhere, but certainly not here and now. I just want to forget it, but you know something, I can't."

"Hey, Ebb. It's me Elmer," he said and laughed. "I came here to fish and camp and have a good time. So let's let the past go! Don't bring it up. This is camping time!"

"I'm for that!" he said. But that memory haunted him since the day he arrived, haunted him in his waking moments, and sometimes terrified him at night. Even now at mid day, he could hear the voices crying out for mercy when there was no mercy to be had.

> *If only they could've pushed it. If only they could have even broken the latch and the lock. If only it opened outward, then this would have never happened. But as it was, one stubborn man insisted that the door swung inward so that the flames might swallow those children!*

Ebb looked around and tried to smile, but the past truly had a harsh grip on his soul. It is a curious thing how old voices wake up within us when we relax out in the wilderness. Seeming to be free, we often find ourselves trapped more than before in the iron cage of our own memory. So it was that these old issues persisted that afternoon as they fished and relaxed along the river's edge until sunset. When they finally started a fire and fried some of the fish on a griddle, he felt glad for the relief from himself.

After they had their bags and tents arranged in a circle, a full moon emerged on the eastern horizon, and as they sat by the camp fire, watching the moon, the old stories started again.

"Look here," said little Billy Hasseler, "I found this cut rock on the bank of the stream."

As the stone was passed around the circle, it came to Ebb who said, "I believe that to be part of a spearhead probably made by an Erie Indian a long time ago. You should keep it. Someday, it might be worth something. You boys, ever heard of the two kinds of Erie?"

"Two kinds of Erie. I know a lot about that from the The Book of Mormon," said Elmer.

"Well having never read the Book of Mormon, I cannot tell you if this particular chapter even got in there or not. So maybe you can answer that question after you hear this tale. But it goes like this. Long, long ago, a trapper turned missionary felt called by God to contact the Erie and try to save their wretched souls. Now Remember, the Erie people numbering some 15,000 lived all around here in fortifications built on hill tops. They had never met a white man, that is, until this fella came along. That was around 1640, or there abouts, before the Iroquois tribes came into these valleys and drove out the last remnants of the Erie. So if you reckon by known dates, this fella was most unusual in that he must have come here close to around 1621 which makes him among the very first explorers. Keep in mind, Columbus himself landed in 1492 which was a mere 129 years before this missionary fella arrived."

"He might have been a Moravian, or one of those French Catholics from Quebec!" said Elmer.

"Maybe he was a Spanish explorer like Cortes," said Billy. "I read about that in school!"

Then Ebb stopped them, "Hold on now. I'm tellin' this! You see, this fella was a solitary wanderer and you probably never read about him in any book because he could not write things down like a normal person can."

"Well, wait a second," said Donny. "How do you know this story, pop, if it wasn't written down."

"Word of mouth, from my own ancestors. That's how I know it to be true," said Ebb

Elmer laughed, "You are sounding more like a Mormon everyday, but go ahead with this yarn of yours."

"So this fella developed a plan to convert the Erie, and it goes like this. He walked into one of their main camps at high noon on a beautiful summer day, and says in a broken native dialect with the help of a translator of course, 'I"ve been sent here in the name of the Great Spirit, and I have brought you great and important gifts.'"

"Well, these folks got right curious because this message struck a cord with certain the people there. It was like something they already knew in their deep memory, but had all but forgotten. So this fella pulls out a carpenter's hammer and a buck saw and some nails. Even more tools, and he spends the whole day showing them how to build things. Together, they built a small table and a push cart. These things made life much easier in the camp. They were happy. It was like they found out something that they long ago forgot. The crude wheel barrow was the most exciting thing. Everybody got a turn pushing that around. At the end of the day, this fella says goodbye, and departs to a hidden place leaving behind all those beautiful tools, and one useless nail."

"So where did he go?" said Billy.

"Oh, he took his canoe up the Chagrin to the lake shore and went east about a mile where no one could spot him and camped there for a month. You see, he wanted the Erie to figure things for themselves, because folks kinda learn better that way. I mean they take ownership and find pride in themselves. So any way, when the next full moon came around, somewhat like that moon you see tonight, he returned and found that same group of the Erie sitting around looking at that one nail."

"And he says, through his translator of course, 'Hey I brought you great gifts from the Great Spirit! What have you done?'

"It split the tribe right in two. Half of them understood his question, and the others became angry. So this here missionary fella picked up the one nail. And he looked around at the Erie and asked them what they were going to do with it. And he turns and says, 'You have seen the tools, you have learned how to work with them, you have built things, and now they belong to your mind. Now, if you want a better life, you must thank the Great Spirit for the gift of your own mind first, and then the rest will come to you. But if all you do is sit around angry and grumpy, then all the tools are worthless.

"Then an angry fellow stood up and said, 'This nail is bent, and dull, and it doesn't work. And you left it here?'

"The missionary looked around and laughed, 'Yes, but there are other nails, and other things beside nails, and you have go find them.

Ebb stopped talking for a moment and stirred the coals of the fire, and tossed a couple of new logs on the fire.

"That's a dumb story," Donny said. "Doesn't even make sense."

"My son," said Ebb as he quit staring at the fire and looked squarely into the boy's eyes, "After watching you dump all that gear in the river this morning for no reason at all, I'm beginning to wonder if you will ever understand even the simplest common sense. You have the gift of life, the tools, the mind, but you act like someone looking at the useless nail. Sometimes, I think, you are just the worst kind of Erie. You need to wake up. Bury your dead, and move on to new things. That's the meaning of my story. The time has come to move ahead, and you have not seen the light. I have nothing more to say!"

"How about you, pop?" said Donny. "Still looking at a worthless nail?"

Elmer stood up, nervous about this story. This father and son were not making sense. "Listen, I'm just a country man, and we are out here having fun. So let's just forgive and forget that river Baptism thing. It was funny. Take it up later. Who cares?"

Ebb stood up. He stared at his son who looked at him. They were both thinking of the Great Fire, but no one present knew about it. The others had not been there. These two could not leave it behind even after two years.

Everyone felt embarrassed for Donny; even somewhat guilty by the way that simple story slipped back into itself and yet kept tugging at their hearts. Donny, more than anyone, felt judged by it. He made a grim face and looked at the others and said, "It's a dumb ending."

"How can it end better?" Ebb asked.

"Take the tools, find a new nail, and make things work," the boy said. "Forget the story."

"Exactly!" said Ebb.

Elmer laughed, "You know, Ebb, if you understand a story like that, you should look into the The Book of Mormon. Why, you're almost a Mormon already. You could come to understand that book. When you did, you'd see that we are all part of one family, all of us, and God wants us to draw together, and do things through the community, and we will, and the sooner the better. " But Elmer did not quite understand the depth of the pain in that story.

Everyone drew silent for a moment.

Ebb retorted, "Maybe everyone's a Mormon already and some of us don't know it yet. Did you ever think of that? Maybe we can never know."

"Well, I ain't goin' touch that one," Elmer said. "Except with a long pole. See, if these are the last days, we got to make the best of each moment."

Ebb stared at the rising campfire. A wheel of flames spun around in Ebb's soul. It flashed with flames of remorse, and it flared with flames of shame. Most of the time, he drove himself forward as he turned his back against it, and tonight he felt that wheel, even as he tried to stop it from burning up his soul. He heard the voices, and no matter where he ran, they followed him. When he spun around, they leaped around in front of him, and even now, they definitely hurt.

Oddly enough, his sometimes angry son understood this better than anyone else. "Grievin" was something the old man did, and his son hated it. The boy hated it more as he came of age because it humiliated him more every day. He understood the man's deep anger about the Great School Fire, but he did not want to tell stories about it. He threw his head back, pushed his lower lip up, and ground his right fist into this left hand. That nail story was about the grieving. Donny knew it, and said nothing.

That night Ebb could not sleep. The old memories had started up again. In his dream, he remembered a neighbor kid called Bernie Horowitz, a raven haired boy with dark eyes who liked to play pinochle. He lived about four doors down from their house on Dulcimer Street. This kid's father worked for the railroad. He was seldom home, so he was reared by his mother and grandmother both of whom ran a bakery on Waterloo Road. Bernie was a genius at cards and numbers and logic. You could see it even when he was yet a little guy. He could begin to figure what the other players had in their hands by counting the cards and telling how they were played. Ebb tried to figure it out, but he would just shake his head and laugh.

When he was only five and half years old, Bernie entered the Elementary school along with many kids who were as much as nine months and three days and twenty one minutes older than him. Bernie would calculate things like that just for fun. He was the youngest in his class, and being young, he frequently found himself face down on the playground while other kids punched his kidneys. This went on until Donny found out about it. Outraged, Donny gathered his friends together and took whoever hurt Bernie and ripped his shirt off in the street after school, and then after a few punches to the face, they threatened the scoundrel to tell anyone He was a Jew, but he was a person also. Soon the big boys left Bernie alone. Kids! Whenever Ebb Collard heard these stories about his son from other parents, he secretly laughed. "My kid wants to take over the world," Ebb said, but he never boasted about it except to Jenny who remained intolerant.

But that night, Ebb saw Bernie somewhere in a smoke filled school, screaming and running ...

> Mrs. Horowitz came running down the street. Hollering, "Where's my Bernie? Has anyone seen my Bernie."
> "Now calm down," said a tall man. "We have a problem here. Someone locked that rear door. Someone sealed those kids in the fire, but we have it open and we are getting kids out and counting heads. Everything will be find."
> "Oh, I know who it was. It was that awful cabinet-maker, Ebb Collard. He's the one all right. He's like a useless nail. Needs to be thrown away. Let's hang him from an oak tree. That's what I say. I saw Bernie by the window on the second floor. Poor brilliant Bernie was frail and small and on the second floor. He choked and cried, and then he died!"
> "Don't know. Don't wanta known! Close it down. Ebb done it to him too!

"No! No! It wasn't me!" Ebb shouted in his dream and then jumped out of the tent.

"Dad. Dad! Wake up! You're having one of those bad dreams!"

Donny was there shaking his father.

Elmer stood up half dressed by the camp fire, "You fellas OK over there?"

Ebb stood still and looked around for a minute. "Yeah, fine. Just a dream. A bad one!"

"It's nothing!" said Donny who protected his father. "He gets these once and a while. It's nothing!"

"Well, if you say so," said Elmer as he looked at Ebb with fear and concern for everyone's safety.

"It's nothing!" said Donny, in that vicious, angry tone that he often spoke.

But it was something. Something frightful.

And the son stood there holding his arm around his father, as he said over and over, "It's nothing!" He meant it as a threat to anyone who came near.

Chapter Ten

Along The Chillicothe Trail

Sometimes to preserve the solitary bliss of the country life you must fight with the wild ferocity of a lynx. Consider the Hasselers. They were ordinary people, just Billy and Alice. A widow for almost five years, she was a pumpkin faced stocky woman with a generous smile and a boisterous voice. She was staunch and blessed. She had to be tough to rear a son alone like she did. He was a tow head kid with freckles and boundless energy. The two of them farmed a nine acre spread on the west side of the Chillicothe Trail. Their farm stood between the Road and the deep woods where Ebb kept his secluded patch of desperation.

They grew tomatoes and corn and had a small peach and apple orchard. Members of the community church frequently helped them at planting and harvesting time when work was arduous. They could not pay much for hired help, but Alice could put together a fine meal, sometimes even twice a day. So when the neighbors helped, she fed them and shared the harvest. Whenever necessary, she had a spare bedroom which she rented out for the needy. She had an old bunkhouse for single men, but they had to be sober, or she would turn them out quickly.

In the years when they fished and hunted, the Collards came to know this little family as if they were part of it.

The Hasseler's two story farm house had a single story kitchen built around an old log cabin, as was common on many old farms. They were poor, but seldom desperate thanks to their friends. Above all else, they attended church regularly and read the The Book of Mormon, along with their King James. Now Alice endured without a man, in part because, in the living room over the fireplace there was a large portrait of a stubborn, fierce man, her husband in a military uniform. Frederick J. Hasseler came from Germany in the eighteen nineties; and though dead five years, his presence did not linger so much as it glared. That face had the ferocity of a lynx, and through it, they somehow bonded to the Collards.

Shortly after the Collards moved into that old Roger's farm house on the edge of the deep woods, Billy established his own inquisitive route there by following the Standing Rock Creek to a point where he ascended a steep hill that opened on a field, and there, with the curiosity of a young boy, for months, he hid along the fence line and carefully studied the activities from a safe distance. Eventually curiosity got the best of him, and the shy boy crossed the field alone and immediately became a friend of that most wary family.

From that moment, Ebb felt obliged to teach the fatherless ten year old everything he knew, and especially, to kindle in the child, the deep secrets of survival in the wilderness. In each young boy, he saw something of himself when he was a youngster. Perhaps most significantly, he let the boy come into the sanctuary where he built that cabinet shop in an abandoned stable, and there amid stacks of board gathered from walnut, curly maple, apple, pear, and even the smaller limbs of the dogwood and black locust, he taught the boy how to fashion a flat board and study the hand print of God that was woven into the grain. Often times, he and the boy would hand plane a piece of walnut or curly, and once smooth , they would wet the surface with mineral spirits or shellac and take it out in the sunlight to study the undulating and iridescent patterns of the grain which spoke of God.'s love. One winter, the boy even made a small serving tray for his mom, and gave it to her on her birthday.

But perhaps the worst example of feline ferocity occurred late in November of 1909. The deer were done breeding and ended their migration. Ebb decided that it was time to teach the boys the fine art of deer hunting. So he summoned them all; the Rodell boys, Chris who was Donny's age, and little Steve who was closer to Billy's age, and Elmer also, since he could tame his own sons better than Ebb who tended to get rough when the boys were unruly. Billy also showed up and brought his favorite hunting knife. They gathered before dawn outside Ebb's wood shop, where the young men received their absolutely critical and necessary instructions. They set their tools on a big bench outside. They had five bows, one long muzzle loaded rifle, Elmer's pistol in a holster, and several bowie knives. So with this arsenal, there was plenty of opportunity for serious action.

As part of the ceremony, Ebb summoned them into the shop where he rubbed their faces with axle grease and made sure they all had adequate camouflage. As he drew triangular lines on Billy's face, he noticed the child's soft light skin and pale blue eyes. He wanted this child to get tough, but he noticed a reservoir of gentleness in the boy that he could not reach. He knew instinctively that this came from his mother who protected him to an excess. So it sparked a lecture from Ebb. It was the single worst lecture ever given to any young boys in the history of Lake County. He said, "Boys, the secret of killing a deer with a bow is an ancient one, known best by the most primitive of men. The idea is to allow the deer to walk into the path of your speeding arrow. You get one shot. If you miss that one shot, the deer will vanish into the brush and run away much faster than you can run. The one shot must hit at the exact spot near the heart in the exact moment when the deer is still. Some prefer the head, but that can be difficult. This is especially true today because there are no big herds like there were twenty years ago. Hunting requires a keen sixth sense. Knowing the right moment, hitting the right spot."

"Am I goin to kill a deer today?" Billy asked.

"Probably not. We will give you a chance, that's all we can do."

"Will you kill one?"

"I've had my fine kills over the years. You just never know. Might be my day. Maybe not."

The boys looked at each other and began to laugh. The whites of their eyes shone bright in the dim light of slowly rising dawn. They looked like wild Erie warriors on the prowl. Donny started to hoop and holler and the others followed.

"Enough of that! All you'll see is the hind end of a deer if you keep up that kind of noise," Elmer said.

And then came that infamous piece of advice. "Let me tell you one more thing," Ebb said as knelt down and pulled out a hunting knife with an eight inch blade. The group circled around him as he looked into each boy's eyes and spoke in a low yet firm voice. "A civilized man hunts with a rifle. A savage hunts with a bow and arrow. But as for the true Erie warrior, he only needs his bare hands and a good knife. That way, he gives the deer a chance." It was a crazy thing to say because somebody just might believe it made sense. He said it to calm the boy's down and get them focused on the seriousness of stalking, but it was definitely a weird expression of that grieving business.

Elmer shook his head and jerked his shoulder's back, "Now let's not be puttin' foolish notions in these kids heads, Ebb! If a wounded deer or any wild animal is still alive, don't be gettin' near it with a knife. Why the deer could whip around and charge at you and even kill you. I have a pistol here in my holster just in case we have to kill a wounded deer. One shot to the head is all it takes." Elmer pulled out the loaded pistol for all to see it. "Enough of this knife hunting! We ain't goin' do that."

"Well here's my point," said Ebb. "Stalking a deer requires absolute stillness, and an absolute urgency about letting the animal come to you quietly. Each of you has to understand the importance of the critical moment. It is what you do before you do the kill. Now let's take up the bows and do some practice shots at that mound of hay I set out by the barn over yonder. This way we will get toned up for the hunt."

Ebb began to feel the wildness of his own youth springing back into his body. The excitement of the young boys did something to him. A flood of memories from his childhood on a farm a long time ago came back to him that morning. He handed Donny a heavy bow he made years ago from an ash tree. It must have tested out at about sixty pounds. Donny said, "Oh no! Not this thing! Not the monster bow!"

Donny tried to set the bow string but could not bend the bow far enough. The others tried and failed. Elmer waved off the exercise because he thought it was somewhat foolish. Then, Ebb pumped his arms and chest and made a sly grimace. He stuck the tip in the ground and wrapped his leg around the lower half of the bow with the end across his instep. Then grabbing the upper end, he bent the bow with his full body and set the string in one swift motion. "See there," he said, "I haven't done that for weeks. Just have to set your mind to it!" Everyone laughed. The boys tried shooting arrows with this tough hunting tool, but only Donny was strong enough to get off a decent shot at the hay stack. Ebb and Elmer both made some accurate shots, while the boys returned to using lighter bows. Finally, Ebb took the big bow, put a sturdy arrow in the notch and pulled it back as far as he could and fired an arrow into the top of a rotted fence post. The post split in half and flakes of shattered wood flew into the air like snow. "That oughta kill a deer," he said and laughed. "Now let's go find one!"

"Better yet, let'em find us!" Billy said.

Everyone laughed as Ebb rubbed Billy's blond hair. "Now you're getting the idea!" he said.

They took the wagon and Finny, the horse, and rode along until they came to M. K. Howell's Store. They left Finny and the wagon there. It was a long two story building that once served as a general store for the whole valley. Up stairs, in the small livings quarters, the elders and his friends taught some of their most sacred scriptures. Elmer, and his family, knew everyone there, for it was even then a sort of sanctuary. The owner agreed to keep an eye on the horse and the wagon while the group hunted.

After they left the store, they proceeded on foot toward an ancient trail, probably used by Erie Indians. There was no road there that morning, only a path in the woods preserved by hunters and wild game. Elmer knew a specific place where a deer often crossed. As they entered the woods they became silent, even trying not to break a twig on the ground or brush against branches. They whispered and made motions with their hands. There were actually too many of them, and there was no coverage since the leaves had fallen only a few months ago. The floor of the forest was littered with dry leaves that crackled at every step. Nevertheless, at a certain turn in the trail, Elmer pointed out a spot where he had often seen a buck come up from the field, climb a slope toward safe ground, and hide in the brush during daylight.

The team circled around and set up a plan. Donny took the big bow and opened it up about two thirds and locked it there with a stick cut by hand from a small maple branch. He then climbed up in a crotch formed by two white oak trees where he set a steel head arrow in the braced bow. The others boys took positions along the trail. Some were high up, others low down to the ground. Elmer had the pistol and went back up the trail about fifty feet, and Ebb took the muzzleloader and went further back to an outpost. They had devised hand signals and did no talking. Two fingers in a V shape meant the buck was climbing the slope. With all in agreement on the plan, they waited for a long time.

High in the trees the last leaves of autumn agitated each other in a light breeze. Squirrels soon descended from the upper limbs and ran over logs searching for acorns. Whenever the sun dipped behind clouds, they felt a chill as if something weird was about to happen. After about one hour, the whole hillside turned gray, and then far down in the field the buck came alone leaping a fence, feeding, surveying, and then advancing gradually up the slope.

Like a pagan god, he raised his head and listened with an intensity that made him one with everything around him. Ebb noticed the vivid way this deer looked at things. He did not seem to be looking at anything in particular, but listening and feeling each thing, he became a sensory mirror to everything and every movement. His very existence resulted from his inward alertness. He saw in each minute movement the possibility for his own instantaneous death; and yet, mysteriously, he thrived on a deep inner peace that guided him along the fragile corridors of brush and limb. As Ebb watched from behind the huge trunk of a soaring tulip tree, he, like most hunters, actually envied the animal he and the group was about to kill. The buck had stealth and mobility that humans wished for. Ebb also knew that one wrong move could ruin the moment. One slight cough and the buck would take flight in the blink of an eye. So he listened, motionless, and watched keenly with full concentration. Slowly, the buck advanced to where Donny sat in the tree. When he was near the boy, Donny released the branch and drew back that powerful bow and held it. Ebb could see the boy's hands trembling mightily. The steel arrowhead focused on a point on the trail where he expected the buck to cross.

Once more, the boy's arm trembled even more. Again all this seemed to take forever as if time itself was suspended in slow animation. The trembling arms waited as the buck nipped at shoots and moved cautiously. For an instant, the buck stopped at the edge of the trail, listened, looked around. This God like creature was being outwitted by Donny who held fast. Then, the buck took about three quick steps into the opening, and stopped. Donny released the bow. The bright and swift arrow surged across the dim lit trail and entered the buck's rib cage slightly behind the right front leg. The animal leaped high, wheeled about, and dropped to its knees for a moment, then rose again and hobbled quickly into the underbrush. Three other arrows followed from the other boys, none hit the animal.

Then in a flash, it happened. Fearing that buck was about to run, Donny dropped the bow and leaped from the tree. With a long bowie knife in his right hand, he plunged into the thicket swinging his knife at the branches, as he screamed like a wild man.

Elmer hollered, "Oh shit!"

Ebb surged forward. He could see Donny's head above the brush as he ran along the trunk of a fallen tree. Elmer began running with his pistol pointed in the air. "Don't go in there! Wait for me! Wait for me!" He shouted and signaled for the other boys to fall behind him. Ebb held up his loaded long rifle and ran as fast as he could. He could see the buck trying to ascend a bank about thirty foot into the brush, and then, to their utter astonishment, everyone saw Donny leap on the buck's back and scream like a wild Erie warrior as he sliced the deer's throat with that knife: then just as quickly, he jumped back away from it and fell into the brush, out of sight.

Ebb stumbled as he followed Elmer into the woods.

"Crazysonofabitch kid!" Elmer yelled as he ran. It took a moment for the men to reach Donny. When they got there, the boy stood back from the animal which now squirmed on the ground with a slit throat. The blood on the boy's shirt was at first frightening. The buck still kicked and churned. Elmer maneuvered around to the animal's head and held his pistol there for a moment. But he did not pull the trigger. Instead, he quietly placed it back in the holster for he could see the blood on Donny's shirt came from the deer.

Soon all the boys came through the woods yelling and hollering and stood around in awe.

"Wha Hoo! Did ya see that?" Donny yelled. "Just like a great Erie warrior! With my bare hands and my knife, I pulled that critter down. What do you think of that, pa? Just like an Erie!"

Elmer said, "Son, that was right foolish. The buck had some life, a lot of life left in him. After that arrow hit, I'd say you are lucky. We are all lucky.

What do you say Ebb?"

"Well, I don't know what to say. I've done dumber things and I'm still kickin'. Son, the shot with the arrow, I watched every second of it. That was beautiful. But like Elmer said, you should've left him run for a bit. Bleeding like that, he would not have gone far. I mean, you never know for sure. But when you see a wild animal in great pain, it's not a good thing to draw near to him like you did. Anyway, it's done. The bow shot was beautiful. He's ours now, boys!"

"Wha Hoo!" they all shouted and laughed as they looked with amazement at the buck.

Elmer lifted both his arms toward the heavens and said, "Quiet everyone! Quiet! Quiet, and listen to me! I mean this. I really mean this. Before these hills were formed, long before these trees took root, the Lord brought forth this animal. Boys, you must never forget that. When the Lord had not yet made the fields, nor the first bits of soil wherein the grass grew, He made this deer you see here before you. Don't ever forget that. When He established the earth and the stars, this deer was there with God. Rejoice in that thought, and let this creature return to his Creator quietly. That's enough violence for one day."

Donny jumped back and shook his head and looked at the others. "But!!... But! I killed it!"

"Only because God gave him to you, Donny! Only because God brought the deer to you!" Elmer said with an authoritative tone. "When you forget that, you don't hunt, you kill your pets. There's a big difference. You may even get killed. I seen it happen!"

Ebb looked around at everyone and said, "Okay, I steered you guys wrong this morning. Elmer's right this time. Listen to what he's tellin' yah. Otherwise we would all be killin' each other. I know that feelin. I fight agin it everyday."

Silence fell over the group. Elmer looked at the deer, then for a moment closed his eyes, and folded his hands. The others watched, and each with their own deep thoughts as the animal lapsed into the arms of his Creator, and departed this world before their eyes.

Then carefully, they pulled the heavy carcass down the hill and set it along the edge of the old Chillicothe Trail. Everyone talked excitedly and made plans for steaks and sausages and jerky. The boys could not wait to tell their mothers. It was Billy's first hunting venture, but surely not his last. With the deer by the side of the road, Ebb walked back to the store to fetch the horse and Wagon. Elmer stayed with the boys, and told them one hunting story after another, and said more than one joyous prayer in an effort to remind those boys that they were ordinary people, and not wild cats. But it did not do much good.

That night, after they got home and Donny went to sleep, Ebb went up to his and Jenny's bedroom and closed the door quietly. Jenny combed her hair by the mirror. A small lantern burned with a pale yellow glow right beside her on the small vanity. Ebb sat on the edge of the bed and pulled off his boots. "You know, Jen, I didn't want to say anything in front of the boy tonight because I don't want to stir up suspicion between him and his friends. But you know, that Elmer did one of the oddest things I've ever seen."

"Well, what odd thing could he do? He's just our friend."

"Well, after we dragged that buck out of the woods and placed him on the wagon, we rode along that old trail to a grove of trees. There was an old rundown barn there and some rusted equipment from somebody's abandoned farm. Anyway, it didn't look like much of anything to me. But Elmer says this was where The Prophet had seen some sort of vision of Jesus and God, the Father. I could not believe that something like that could happen in such a rundown place. Anyway, the next thing he does is jump off the wagon, kneel down by this tree stump. Looked like a tree had been felled there a few years ago; and there, believe it or not, he says this awesome prayer of thanks. Now, does that make sense, or am I goin' crazy?"

"Well, Ebb, maybe it is just sacred to Elmer, that's all. Maybe he goes there often for some special reason. Maybe that's how he spotted that deer in the first place. It's just probably a favorite place for him. Something like that place where you go all the time, by that walnut tree in the ravine. Besides that, from what you told me about the hunting story, I think Donny might have scared him quite a bit. Elmer's a sensitive man."

"I guess you're right. He sure knew that buck would come through around nine o'clock. Yes, he knew the exact spot all right. Just seems weird.

A grown man seeing Jesus and God by a run down shack in the woods." He laid his head back on the pillow and rubbed his eyes.

"Well maybe, it wasn't run down seventy years ago when all the Mormons were here. Things change over time. We all change. Anyway, we got to get up early. You know Alice! She will be up here at sunrise with all those friends of hers, and we will be grinding and packing sausage and smoking meat all week. She told me they goin' bring up fresh pork just to soften venison. And then she said one of her friends will bring spices and things to marinate some Slovenian sausage."

"It'll be a fine time. Just hope no one kneels down by my old busted up rain barrel and starts seein' Jesus risin' out of the cistern. That sort of thing makes me nervous."

"Now, Ebb, stop it! That part of the woods was a sacred place for Elmer, that's all. Just somethin' special to him. Besides, I've been thinkin' and prayin' lately. I think I'm about to join that Community of One Church. Right now, they are the only true friends I have in this world."

Ebb covered his eyes with his right hand. It was a gesture of spiritual confusion, as if all his memory and sense of reality whirled around like a merry go round inside his head. For a moment, he saw the buck once more only this time in his imagination, much like ancient hunters who drew images on the walls of caves. He remembered his own advice given to Billy. Ancient, probably primeval, planted in the heart of man since the beginning of time. For there is an art in letting something cross over into your line of sight. It's a gift of some sort. It implies that life owns you more than you own it. But as you hang there in a kind of delicate balance, if things tip the wrong way as you make a wrong move, you could lose the deer. So maybe Elmer's spontaneous prayers made sense. The planet itself belonged not to man but to God.

Somewhere in the back of his mind, Ebb wanted to feel that same kinship, but he did not quite understand it. It was as if he had been cut off from himself. It only brought tears to his eyes, and as he drifted off to sleep, he once again remembered The Great Fire...

Mike Wilson was a short stalwart kid, every inch a pioneer, an adventurer. He lived only three blocks from their house in Collin Wood. To make himself useful, little Mike delivered newspapers. "The Plain Dealer" sought hardy kids like him. He could wake up at four in the morning, throw the morning's news up and down the streets fairly accurately, and still make it to school on time. In any city at any given time, one out of five hundred kids must exist who could land a paper on a porch without breaking anything. But they never saw themselves as heroes. Ebb knew the boy, knew his parent, knew folks at St. Mary's Church even though the kid seldom attended it. Mike was handsome. He had developed his muscles both in arms and legs. The girls liked him, other boys feared him. In the third grade, reading and writing drove him nuts, but he hung in there. The text had to go fast, the numbers had to come quickly, and if they did not, Mike pitched the books quickly, and ran out to the playground.

He was Huck Finn on wheels. He needed directions and reasons and at least one strong adult who could slow him down, and yet it seemed there was no one equal to the task. He spent many hours standing with his face to corner in the fourth grade.

Donny Collard was one of the guys he wanted to knockdown. The two boys had boundaries that they dared not cross. For when they he did, they would soon be found tumbling on the ground throwing hard punches. In some ways, they were the mutual incarnation of each other.

It was in 1906, when they got into their big fight. Donny had written an essay in which he said that Abraham Lincoln was not as great a president as George Washington because George fought in the Revolutionary War, and Abe fought in some silly war. The teacher liked the paper. It was hard for Donny to write what he did, but even harder to read it in front of the class. Some students laughed. Young Mike Wilson was one of them. After school out in the street, he called Donny a series of bad names, most which added up to a modern day queer. The boys argued and then began exchanging blows. Nobody knew what they were arguing about. The subject itself was meaningless. But the boys latched into each other, Wilson got the worst of it. Both of theirs shirt were ripped, their eyes blackened. When it was over, Donny stood up, spat on the ground, and declared a truce. But there was no truce. They would remember that moment for the rest of their lives.

Kids going to school do things extremely important.

When Ebb got word of the fight, he laughed quietly. He said, "My son wants to take over the world." It was some sort of joke that all parents have. Some sort of dream. But the word got around. Next day Jim Wilson, appeared on the porch with Mike who looked somber and roughed up. He said, "Your son has a nasty attitude and I think you encourage it in him. This has to stop. When I heard about this fight, I gave my son a good lickin', and I told him I want no more of this. But it takes two to stop a quarrel. So I want to hear an apology from that boy of yours."

"Donny," Ebb hollered at the boy who was in the house finishing his dinner. "Come over here right now. What did I tell you about that fist fightin!"

"You told me to take over the world," Donny said and then he caught the back of Ebb's swift right hand against his mouth.

"Don't be a smart guy around me. Son, tell these folks you're sorry. Let's see you boys shake hands. Tell him it's not goin' to happen again."

So the boys shook hands and declared a truce. It lasted until the day of the Great Fire when the end came. Mike never came out of the school, and Jim Wilson blamed Ebb for it. That old grudge would never go away.

Kids. Memories. Neighbors.

"I want to forget it all!" Ebb mumbled in his sleep. "Go away you wicked voices! Erase that day of the Great Fire! Hang on there, son, we are comin' for you. Hang onto to those moorings. We are climbing the Fire ladder now!"

Ebb's moaning woke up Jenny. She looked over her shoulder at her husband and knew what it was, "*The grievin.*'" She nudged him with her elbow hoping that would shake him out of it. He rolled over and pretended to go back to sleep. He could not forget what happened on that day.

Chapter Eleven

A Reasonable Offer

From the moment he met the man at the door that morning, Paul had his suspicions about Crandall. For one thing, the man hovered about the secretary desk as if it were his own when, in fact, Paul and his wife were the actual owners. Worse yet, he did not allow others to touch or even breath on the thing because the oil from their hands or moisture from their breath could mar the finish. One thing he did was good. He wore clean white cotton gloves when he opened and closed the cabinet doors. This was more than a thoughtful gesture, but the act of a professional.

Paul appreciated the white gloves. But what truly aroused his suspicion was the boards on the back. These he had been told by his wife were taken from an older cabinet and put into place in such a subtle and careful manner that no one could tell the difference. In fact, the only people that knew this were Crandall, Susan, and now Paul. These old boards and the rusted nails that held them in place provided strong evidence for the older date, and therefore added significantly to the value.

All these things bothered Paul, but nothing bothered him more than the fact that some key to the cabinet was possibly concealed in a subtly hidden drawer known only by the evasive and yet to be seen Mr. Hasseler. This piqued his curiosity until it came to a crescendo around three o'clock that afternoon. Fed up with delays, he went up to Susan and said, "My dear, I have the answer to the truth about this piece."

"What truth?" she said.

"I believe there is yet another drawer or sliding panel or some sort of mark on this cabinet and I'm going to find it myself. I'm going to get my own white gloves, my own tapping and nudging and probing tools, and I 'm going to find this secret heart of this thing. Yes, I know I can do this"

"Well, you have to ask Crandall."

"Why? You told me it is yours and what is yours I have an interest in it. Don't I?"

"Well, yes, but I hired him to do the appraisal as well as to negotiate the sale. He's an expert."

"Well, I'm going to talk to him right now. Have you heard anymore from our friend in Utah?"

"Not a word. He has my number though. I expect a call anytime."

"Okay, this baby's mine," said Paul as he rubbed his palms together and started across the room to where Crandall was showing some guests an old antique clock that was up for sale. Paul interrupted their conversation and told Crandall his plans in very blunt terms. All the man said was that he could not stop him from going forward with his tools, but he had to watch and document the process carefully. If something broke or was even scratched in the slightest way, it could devalue the piece. Paul reassured him that nothing bad would happen, and then he went out to his car and returned in about thirty minutes with a small plastic tool box, six pairs of white gloves similar to the ones Crandall had been wearing, and a small step ladder. Thanks to the delay of Mr Hasseler, Paul was now his own self proclaimed expert.

The amusing event that followed went on for almost an hour. People stood around and watched. All along, they offered enough suggestions to aggravate a saint. Paul climbed on the step ladder that was in front of the cabinet, went over every inch of the top with a flash light and a small plastic hammer, taping in order to hear hollow sounds, then looking for any little nail, screw, or wooden device that might release a hidden drawer. He removed the flame shaped finial on the center of the top and even looked down into the hole where he saw a small pilot hole made by a drill. He tried wiggling the crown molding which appeared to be loose, but it was also secured by a dovetail joint. On and on he went, pulling, probing, tapping, and wiggling. In about thirty minutes, he had every removable drawer and shelf and bracket scattered out on three tables in front of the entire group. He had fortunately taken the trouble to label everything. After all, he was an auto mechanic. He separated the secretary on top and placed it by itself on top of a dining table. He then tipped it backwards and forwards looking for the secret panel.

All the while he did this, Crandall held a pad in his hands and took copious notes of this entire assault on this old and priceless antique. He continually shook his head saying over and over, "I did all this in my shop, and found nothing."

Paul then asked five men to tilt the lower desk section on its back carefully. They placed it on another table by itself, and he went over every board on the bottom just as much as he did the top. Everyone was amazed by the crude workmanship on the structures underneath. The dovetailing on the drawers was almost perfectly and consistently hand cut by a skilled person. Many tenons went clear through the end of mortises and were pegged by small square pegs inserted from behind. But the underside looked as if it had been hastily chopped with an ax.

Crandall made notations and added, "The old cabinetmakers did not waste time polishing those parts of the cabinet that were unseen by the end user. Like the rest of us, they had families to feed. They needed to get things done."

After Paul finished he stood in front of the scattered display. There were about thirty small drawers on one table, a stack of four large drawers on another, boards for shelves on another. The top itself was laying on its back on a large table. Every drawer or shelf had numbers that matched other numbers on the cabinet. Paul stood back with his hands on his hips and said, "There is no doubt in my mind at this point. There is only one secret drawer, and we already saw that earlier today. This thing has no name on it anywhere and no hidden drawer. I'm going to concede, in my humble opinion, that it was made over two hundred fifty years ago, most likely in New England. That's it." He looked around at the curious faces of the crowd, "Anybody else want to try it? Anybody have another opinion?" he asked.

"I think you have proved your point," said the man with the big gold ring. "As I said earlier, Mr Hasseler is not going to change our opinion. What ever became of him anyway? Shouldn't he have called by now?"

Susan spoke out over the group, "Let me assure you, he will contact us soon. He is probably waiting for the next flight. He might even be on another flight. Just hold on until we hear from him. The last time I contacted him was last night about eight o'clock. He promised me he would be here before six today."

"This is getting ridiculous," Paul said, causing the whole group to begin mumbling and arguing all over again. "Let's get this over with. Let's agree together that it was made before the year 1800. That's a safe guess and long enough to insure its value as an original. Now let's put a value on it, some sort of opening bid, and we will settle for that. Then we can move on to an auction. Does anyone here disagree with that?"

There was a long pause, and then Crandall spoke, "I think it is a reasonable request, but the owners and I must confer in private in order to decide how we want to proceed from this point. One thing is important, we need to allow the bidding process to continue in the form of offers taken over the next ten to thirty days so that the bidders will have time to compare other cabinets of this kind and make reasonable assessments."

The man with the gold ring lifted his right hand over his head and said, "Well, I know where I am coming from on this. I will make an opening offer right now. I offer you, the current owners, twenty thousand dollars right now today. I know an authentic thing when I see it. This cabinet is between two hundred and two hundred fifty years old, and I want to own it!"

Susan became jittery when she heard this offer. She suspected that her husband would jump at it just to get this business over with. She looked at his face. He seemed confused.

Paul looked back at her and, in low whisper, asked, "What happened to the one hundred thousand price tag?"

Susan said, "Now wait. Wait! Wait! We need to see what interest is here, and what kind of money. Just wait. So now we have a firm offer. This is the beginning of a firm deal. It is not the end. We have not accepted this offer. Not yet. My husband, Crandall, and I must talk alone about this."

"It's good for thirty days. Guaranteed!" said Harper. "I know my business."

Crandall looked at both of them and then at other faces in the room. After a moment, he said, "Ladies and gentlemen, that's fair. Let it be known by all present that we have a firm offer of twenty thousand dollars from Mr. Harper. The owners and I must confer in private at this point. But we have a firm offer, do we not?"

"Oh, indeed, you do," said the man with the big gold ring. "I know my cabinets. My twenty thousand dollar offer is good for thirty days. After that, forget it."

"Well, with that before us, I suggest we all retire." Crandall's lemon face assumed a dour smile but he retained his equanimity. "Let us return, that is, all who are still interested in this sale, at six thirty this evening. But if you do not mind, Mr. Harper, I prefer that we have this offer in writing. Meanwhile, we shall put this scattered cabinet back together exactly as it was. Let us all get some dinner. We will think this over and return at six thirty. Also any other interested parties, please sign this guest register, so we can keep everyone informed about this as well as other items for sale. The owners and I have some issues to discuss in private. Thank you all. We have a firm offer of twenty thousand dollars! Wonderful!"

Excitement was in the air. A deal was about to crystallize. For now, there was only one serious hurdle to the closing of this venture. Hasseler. Who was he? What did he know?

Part Two
Creation and Destruction

He who binds himself to a joy
Does its winged life destroy;
But he who kisses the joy as it flies
Lives in Eternity's sunrise.

- William Blake

Chapter Twelve

A Letter of Invitation

Two years passed. Hard years. The tools in the stable gathered dust and rust. The stuff of life piled up on the benches. Boxes. Old clothes. Hoes and shovels and wagon parts. Even the latest inventive trash, a broken gasoline engine. Canoe paddles and fishing rods commingled in one corner. The shop of dreams became a dreary warehouse filled with junk of dubious value.

Then in the final days of winter, a disturbing letter arrived at the Collard Farmhouse.

As if a testimony to lost souls, it was left in the mail box on Chardon Road, almost three quarters of a mile from the house itself which was too remote for the postman, who refused to trek back there either in winter or summer. Donny brought it to his mother on his way home from school. He almost forgot to give it to her. When she opened it and read it quietly, tears came to her eyes.

March 1, 1912

Dear Ebb And Jenny,

Hope this note finds you well and happy. I am writing to remind you that it has been four years since the tragedy. Things have changed here. A new school has been built. They built a memorial garden where the old school stood. Life has resumed so much that you would not recognize the place. The officials are planning a memorial service, and they want me to come. I would sure be lost without the two of you to help me get around. My eyesight is so bad now that I have to hire someone to read to me, even to write this note to you while I speak out loud. I know you have your reasons for not wanting to come here, but the Lord knows better than anyone what you should do.

You must come and see what has been done. I'm still at the same old house. Lay aside all your anger and grief for my sake, and in the name of Jesus come and see us.

Love
Uncle Henry

Jenny set the note down on the small table beside her rocking chair and began to wipe her eyes with a handkerchief. They had no phone, no electricity. For years, they lived in a state of isolation. They taught themselves to tolerate the past by forgetting it. But this simple note forced memories to rise up like an enormous thunderstorm.

Ebb never talked about this business to anyone. He hated those memories. He felt he could never separate himself from them. And they hung around day after day in his mind like a stalled storm. He hated himself for even having an imagination.

She understood this storm better than he did. She called these memories his "grievin." And she resented it. It was a persistent grief for her too.

When Ebb came home that night, she waited until he washed up and settled for the evening. He had been working on the Morrison's mansion all winter, building more and more cupboards; the owner there loved cupboards. It was good money, even though getting over there was not always easy with the snow and all.

She came into the living room, which was lit by several oil lanterns. Ebb sat by the fire place splitting up kindling for the next morning. "Ebb," she said with a quiet voice, " Uncle Henry wrote us a note. Says he wants us to come down to Collin Wood and visit. Here," she handed it to him quietly.

He read it, folded it up and put in his shirt pocket. "Four years and it seems like yesterday," he said. "I said years ago I would never return to that place. I hate it. I hate the memory of it. What do you think? Has the time come to return?"

"Well, we don't have to go," she said as she placed a hand on his shoulder.

"Huh! I've thought about this trip for years. But lately, I keep thinkin' about it differently. Elmer got his hands on one of Mr. Morrison's older *automobiles*. It's a strong machine. I need him to go. Reason being, he is prayin' man, and I'm not. I'll talk to him in the mornin'. I never have explained any of that business to anyone around here. They don't even know what happened back there in Collin Wood four years ago."

"I'm goin' with you Ebb."

"I didn't say I was goin'. I was just thinkin' I could."

"Fine," she said, "Let's take Donny too. Time he learned some things."

He reached up and held her hand for a moment and then resumed splitting the kindling as he studied the flames in the fire place. Over the years, it had become easier to look at an open fire. He could look and not feel terror. But he could look and still hear the shrill voices and the moaning.

He let her hand slip away. He never said much more that evening. Once again, just as she knew he would, he started grieving all over again. Only this time, he managed it better than he did in the old days. He had come a long way in the last four years. First, there was that impressive business of Feargus and his family. That got him to thinking better of himself. Then there was the farm. That gave him plenty to do. Then numerous fishing and hunting excursions with the young boys revitalized him by reminding him of the joy and innocence he once knew as a child.

Slowly, perhaps reluctantly, he had learned over the years how to respect someone who prayed, even though he himself found it impossible to pray. Those many prayers of his friend Elmer instilled in him, by a sort of osmosis, a recognition that the tragic sensibility was at the core of not just his, but every human life. So much so, that he came to realize this grief was normal; that different people were the same at the center of their being; that all people were set apart from nature; and perhaps most importantly, it was the grief that bonded them, and made them human.

Something was happening to Ebb. His old anger began crumbling, even as he drew strength from feelings he could not express in words. He felt inklings of an inner power beyond any power he had known before. He found comfort in that.

The next morning, he talked to Elmer and a plan was arranged.

The following morning, Ebb was out in the yard early in the morning. He was burning branches that had fallen in winter. He heard the *automobile* before he saw it as it moved over the horizon with swift power of one hundred horses. A covey of quail sprang up from the field and flew in all directions. Ebb shook his head, "In the back country, *horses* are the way to travel, not by machine." When one of these inventions came down a country trail, the noise of the engine itself was as disturbing as it was foreign. Smoke, often mixed with dust, billowed behind and settled on the crops. It was like a nightmare, or even the apocalypse! This *horseless* carriage shocked the sensibilities. A machine perpetually propelling itself over a horse and carriage trail? The very idea inspired not only wonder and fear but also laughter.

As the *"carriage"* came over the hill, he saw Billy, perched high on the back seat of that canary yellow 1907 Peerless touring car., his scarf blown about by the wind. There was Elmer at the wheel and Chris, his oldest son. He waved his hand and the boys responded in kind. Ebb was not quite expecting the boys, but he could see they were thrilled by the speed and power of that car. Ebb wondered, *"Maybe the power of that artificial invention would make the trip an adventure in itself."* But would it help him transcend that endless grief that that filled the basin of his soul, and occasionally spilled over as rage against life? Hopefully. He wasn't sure.

Elmer pulled the car into the driveway and stopped with a jolt, but he left the motor idling. "What do think of this baby!" he shouted as he stepped down from the running board.

Ebb pulled off his gloves and leaned his rake against a tree. "Amazing thing these big cars! Are you sure we can make it all the way to Cleveland?"

"Not a problem."

Soon Jenny and Donny came out and climbed aboard the back seat with the two boys. Ebb took the front seat behind the windshield and next to Elmer. The car had a long canvas top that flapped when the air hit it and made a noise something like kite on a windy day. Elmer wheeled the car around in the yard jumping over a pile of leaves and crushing a few dried plants before he got it lined up on the trail and took off. Soon, it accelerated with such speed that the shocked passengers could not refrain from laughter. It was a brisk, cool morning so everyone bundled up in heavy coats and hats. Unlike the Model T, the Peerless was a rich man's machine; but this one was five years old, and it belonged to the Morrison family, who had six other automobiles. They owned most of the Inner Urban, which was an electric streetcar business in those days. Elmer and Ebb both worked on the family's country home. They were one of many wealthy families who had both country estates and large homes in Cleveland.

It was sixteen miles to Cleveland. As they followed the Chardon Road, they sometimes clipped along at fifty miles per hour and more than once hit a rock or a hole which set everyone to laughing except the driver himself, who maintained a stern and sober face. When they came to a long hill that descended down to the Euclid Avenue, Elmer shifted the car into low range so that the engine would serve as a break. The car sputtered and backfired as it came down and merged with the traffic. Everyone laughed and hollered, except Elmer who prayed hard.

It did not take long for them to find the old school yard. Following Ebb's instructions, Elmer brought the Peerless to a stop on the street, "Now didn't that there school house burnt down around here somewhere years back?" he asked as they stopped in front of a beautiful garden.

Ebb got out and stood speechless on the sidewalk. Everything had changed. There was a new school built behind where the old one stood, and in front of it, there was a beautiful garden with walk ways and a memorial plaque. Since it was March, nothing was in bloom nor were there any green leaves or grasses; but they could see what had been done. Most of all he saw the names written on the bricks.

"It burnt down four years ago this week on Ash Wednesday. One hundred seventy two students burnt to death on that day, and three adults died also. I know all about it. I was here at the time. Donny was on the third floor. He remembers it all too well. He was tryin' to save his buddy Mike Wilson, but we don't talk about that much do we son? We knew every one.

But let's not go into the garden now. Let's move on to see Uncle Henry. He lives around the corner from here."

"Well, I'll be darned. You never told me about this. I remember that fire. I mean I lived out in Lake County at the time. Some friends of mine lost their daughter in that fire. They say it was terrible. People stood outside in the street and watched the children as they leaped from windows, on fire no less. Through the windows parents watched their children burning inside. They say somebody built the doors so that they opened inward, and the kids piled up against them so that they could not get out. That's what people say. That's where most of the kids burned right by the front and rear doors."

"Move on," said Ebb as he climbed back into the car. Jenny gently grabbed his shoulder. Ebb brushed her hand off, "Elmer, I've got something I have to tell you."

"Now, Ebb just calm yourself. It wasn't your fault," said Jenny.

"Its ok, Jenny. It's all right. I'll get it all out right now!" Ebb almost shouted as his face turned red. "Stop this damn car and listen to me."

Elmer lurched ahead then abruptly stopped. "What on earth has gotten into you?"

"Almost a year before the fire, I was hired to rebuild those doors because they were weathered and worn out. All the doors swung out and I made sure they worked quite well. I took them down and planed them by hand. I put longer and stronger screws in the hinges. I tested them carefully. A school door gets a lot of abuse, and when storms came off the Lake they sometimes blew the doors back and pulled the hinges loose. Lake Erie is only a few blocks away, and high winds ripped up doors all the time. At that time, we discussed the idea having the doors swing inward for that reason. On most homes, the doors open inward. These opened outward. I put a latch operated lock on the inner doors because kids had fooled with the old lock. They had been locking each other out as a prank. I did what they asked me to do. But something went wrong that morning. The janitor said he opened the doors as soon as he saw the fire. Anyway when the kids came running down the rear stairway, they piled up in the stairway and burned to death. They never got to the door.

"My friend JimWilson's son died in that fire. To this day, he tells everyone that I killed all those kids because I made the doors open inward. It never happened that way. Now has everyone heard that? Do you want me to repeat it? Do you wonder why I'm the way I am?"

"Ebb dear, now, it was not your fault. You did what you thought was right at the time," Jenny began to cry as she pressed a firm hand on Ebb's shoulder.

The boys became frightened. Donny particularly withdrew into anger. He pounded his right fist into his left hand, as his eyes glared. "Up on the third floor, Mike found a way to come across the ceiling by swinging on a board nailed to the rafters. He was comin' toward me hand over hand. I reached out and hollered to him when he lost his grip. I looked into his eyes as he plunged into the flames below. I see his face everyday since. He was my best friend."

"Well, now," Elmer said, "I wish you two had told me this before, but you know something like this, well, it's just one of those things that happens in this life. Surely, the door worked for years. Somebody probably locked it thinking nothing would happen on that morning. As I recall, the whole building was a fire trap to start with. Why that fire swept right up the wooden stairways as if they were chimneys."

"Well, some say I'm the fool who fixed the door that killed the kids! They had a mob lookin' for me," Ebb said as he pointed at himself with his finger to dramatize his deep anguish. "Let's move on to Uncle Henry's. I haven't seen the man for four years. Now you know why I don't come down here."

"Well, we have to get this right. Sounds to me like you need to talk to the Lord," said Elmer.

"Not right now," said Jenny because she knew more talk would just escalate the whole business.

"Move on," said Ebb as he motioned for Elmer to pull ahead. "Uncle Henry lives right around the corner. I'm beginning to regret this trip."

The three boys sat stoned faced. Not one of them knew what to say. No one did for that matter.

Elmer drove around and stopped at a small house.

Henry Gold was not a colored man, but something about him seemed to make him a man of color. He was a lean, tan skinned fellow with long silken fingers. What hair he had was gray and combed flat. His lips were thick and his nose long and his flesh was so thin you could see the bones underneath. When the group knocked at his door, he hollered out for them to come in; and they filed in and took seats across from him. It was a dim room in a bungalow which though small was large for the lot that surrounded it. Henry sat beside a tall green Victorian gas lamp. Next to him on a walnut Eastlake table, a big black Bible rested on a somewhat yellow doily. There was an odor of soiled clothes and a full garbage pail. The fragrance of a life being endured.

From the smile on his face and the slight laughter in his voice, one would think he had a twinkle in his eyes, but there were no eyes now. That part of life had darkened some years ago. So he wore dark glasses over the stone cold portals and nodded his head almost constantly as he listened.

Henry was Jenny's uncle. He was part Iroquois with the rest of him gathered up from that rough sort of folk who blazed trails through the wilderness and eventually settled in the city broke and tired and full of the wisdom that keeps a man alive well into his eighties. Ebb introduced everyone in the room, and each shook hands with Henry who never stood up once. They talked small talk mostly about the farm itself and the crops they had. Then ever so gently, Henry chided Ebb for moving into the country. He said, "Seems to me life would be terribly lonely out there on the edge of the woods. Beautiful and yet lonely. Especially at night, and even worse in a hard winter. I lived like that when I was child, and also when I farmed out in Thompson. But Lords knows, it's a hard place for a woman. And you, sir. Elmer's your name, right? Have you many friends?"

"I have friends. I have a wife and three boys, and a daughter. Most of my friends are church members. We help each other a lot. We watch over each other. It's part of our faith."

"And what faith might that be?"

"We have our own small church called The Community of One."

"You don't say. I'm Baptist myself. Most folks live around here are Catholic," said Henry. "Do you believe that Jesus died for the sins of the whole world and rose again on the third days and ascended into heaven as a promise for all?"

"That's for certain."

"Good for you. God bless you, my friend. Welcome to the neighborhood. What say you, Ebb? Have you softened your views?"

Ebb rubbed his chin and looked at the others. "What is this Sunday School? I read the Bible. I read the book of Mormon sometimes. It's all the same. But my beliefs shift around. Freedom, that's my religion. Freedom from the ill opinions of a sick society!"

"OOO," said Henry, "felt some sting in those words. Same old Ebeneezer Collard!"

Everyone laughed at that comment, even Henry, who was the only one who could chide Ebb, and get away with it. He loved to do it.

"Everybody wants freedom," Henry went on nodding his head. "But are you really free? I know that you and I liked to tinker with woodworking. It's in our blood. Yours more than mine. I remember some of those things you built for Mr. Stonefeller. Mighty fine. But you can't tell me you find time for that out there in the country. You got to plant, you got to cultivate and weed the garden, you got to harvest. You got to repair fences and buildings. Then you got to can and store food for winter. Come Saturday night when your worn out, you fool around sharpening your blades, and for what? So you can start the same old thing the next day. That's country life. Did it for years."

Ebb leaned forward, "Well, remember those old drawings for that old secretary desk that my grandfather gave to me when I was kid?"

"That Koladari project. You still got those old tools?" Henry said with a big smile.

"Yep. Everything right there in a stable behind my house waiting to be reborn. I fiddle with it once and a while, most often in the Winter, when I have no work. Junk piled up in there right now, but I don't forget it. No sir. I'm goin to build that sucker some day."

"Well, I'll be darn. Right proud to hear that! That was a beauty! Listen, I've been thinkin' about that. You know I'm done doin' any woodwork. Since my eyes are gone, can't do much of anything. On a good day, I walk around in circles. But I got some boards back there in my shed. Nice clean maple boards, which if you worked down, you could put them in the cabinet. Some of them came out of the old school after the fire. Fine boards. Survivors of the flames. You are welcome to 'em."

Ebb moved forward in his chair and sat bolt up right. "I hate that place."

"You know Ebb, I don't appreciate that. I mean you and I know where you're comin' from, but you did nothing wrong there. Nothin' at all. Besides that, remember what the Good Book says. Elmer here will tell where to look it up in the Bible. Goes like this: 'You have heard that it has been said of old, Thou shalt love your neighbor, and hate your enemy. But I say unto you, Love your enemies, bless them that curse you, do good to them that hate you, and pray for them who despitefully use you, and persecute you. For the Lord makes the sun to shine on the evil and on the good, and sends rain on the just and the unjust.'"

"Amen," said Elmer. "Many of my friends and family suffered grievously. Many died in Missouri and on the plains for their faith, but they moved ahead, praying for their enemies. If you don't do that, your own anger eats you up, and you die with a bitter soul. Amen, I say to that."

"See there, your friend knows you better than you know yourself," said Henry nodding and smiling. "Let me tell you somethin, Ebb. Things is changed around here since you were here four years ago. A lot of people been prayin'. A lot of thinkin' and prayin' still goes on. Today, the general opinion is that old wooden school building was designed and built wrong from the start. Soft pine supported those stairwells that were built like wooden chimneys. The wind blew hard that day. Soon as they opened those doors, that place went up in flames in ten minutes. Those kids never had a chance. They never even got to the door. Most suffocated in the hallway."

Just then, Jenny came in from the kitchen with a tray of cookies and tea. She stopped before the men and the boys. "Sounds like you fellas having a serious conversation here?"

"Hold on woman, set the tray down gently. Now what are you tryin to say, Henry?" Ebb said.

"You heard it. The building was a fire trap."

"But what about the group that blamed me, that lynch mob led by Jim Wilson? What happened to them?"

"Some of those folks still around. That was mostly an emotional search for a scapegoat. After they thought about it, after they prayed about it, most of them let it go. Didn't make sense?"

"For four years, four years, I've lived in fear of them! Everyone said that fire was my fault."

"I know," said Henry. "But the community failed, not any one person. The community. That's all over."

Ebb drew silent as he motioned for everyone to partake of the cookies.

"Well, that's just talkin'! That's all! I know better," said Ebb. "That's why Elmer's here. He has a country religion, a faith in the earth, a faith in a community of believers. I'll take those boards. I don't exactly know why, but I hear what your saying. Great thought for Sunday School, but has no real use in the bitterness of this miserable life. Cause the folks who preach it most, believe it the least!"

Henry smiled. "There you go."

"Well," said Elmer, "Everyone has heard about this woodworking project. You know I might make a suggestion. It just popped into my mind for no reason. But I know where there is some fine walnut. It was milled for the Temple in Kirtland years ago, but they never needed it. Ebb, I feel I should let you have some of that because whenever you talk about building this cabinet in your stable, your soul changes. It's almost as if God wants you to build this thing. Does anyone else sense that?"

Henry smirked. "Huh! Of course. It's an atonement. Doing something to get back in God's graces. You need all the help you can get when you decide to do that. I'd welcome those boards, if I were you," said Henry as he stood up for the first time holding on to an old cane.

"I'll consider it," said Ebb.

"Consider it nothing!" said Henry as he moved slowly. "Accept them as a gift from our Savior. Enough of this. Let's go over by the new school yard. I was right there on the day those children died. No one! No one ever wanted that awful fire to happen. We all sinned on that day. Yes sir, the whole town sinned on that day. Folks see it differently now, than they did four years ago. All of us were at fault on that day. The school was beautiful, but it was a firetrap."

When Ebb reached to guide Henry, he felt a deep blessing come from the man to him. Something was ending, something new had started. It was like the end of a long lonely road. The cloud of self torment that had hung over him for years began to drift away. He did not know why or how, but he knew it was beginning to happen. He felt now as if he had a good reason to work on the cabinet. He could not explain why. He just knew it. When he went out the door, guiding the slow moving old man, he smiled and started to laugh. Something was happening to him that he did not yet fully understand.

"Yep, Elmer, I'll show you where those children burned. We all sinned on that day. The whole town sinned." Henry kept his head up as he descended the stairs with that long wooden cane. He never stopped talking all the way back to the Memorial Garden.

Chapter Thirteen

Ash Wednesday

MARCH 3, 1912

The Memorial Garden had been built on the foundation of the ruined school. The flowers literally grew out of ashes of the deceased. The walk in the garden followed the outline of the first floor with an almost morbid exactitude. There were markers listing the names of the children. It was a shocking reminder of the tragedy. Ebb and Jenny had never seen the garden before this day. It was March, the air was cool, and no flowers bloomed.

They did not bring the car. They walked over slowly. Ebb trembled as he surveyed the scene. Uncle Henry began telling the story to Elmer, but Ebb stopped him, "No, I'm sorry," he said. "I can't let you do this. I want to tell Elmer this story. You can fill in the details later. I have never talked about this horrible tragedy with anyone. For years, night after night, I can never forget what happened here. It all happened so quickly in one hour on Ash Wednesday at 9 A.M. And many, many people blamed me. They said I hung the doors wrong. But it was never true."

Old Henry broke in and said. "Okay, Ebb and Elmer stand over here. Here Donny you guide me around son. Your dad wants to talk. First time. First time's a blessing. Jenny let me hold your hand too," the old man smiled and spoke in a soft voice. "The rest of us just follow. Let the man talk. Just follow."

They walked together slowly, listening.

"The event that happened here shook every religion in the world down to its foundation. It was as if for one hour God ceased to exist. It hurt people so bad some died, and it will hurt as long as it will be remembered.

"People have to dig deep into their souls to find the beauty in it, but it was there. Yes, the beauty was there. As always, there were many heroes on that day. So let me tell you in a prayer from a man who forgot how to pray. I was there. I too helped pull out the burned, the frightened, and the dead. Afterwards, I too knelt down and wept. I remember it all. It went like this:

"It was a cold and windy morning. The gray sky hung overhead like a tent. It extended all the way across the Lake. An easterly wind howled along the streets of Cleveland. It poured its invisible force down Euclid Avenue, down Superior, pushed its way along Lake Shore Boulevard toward the village of Collin Wood. It whirled around the outside of the wooden doors of the school. It slipped under the weather seal on the rear door where it whistled through small crevices. Whirr! Whirr! It sang as it entered the vestibule and then diminished as it rubbed against the second set of interior doors. Whirr! Whirrrr!

"The wind chill in Cleveland can be costly. Coal to heat the big steam boiler burned almost continuously from mid November until the end of March. On that day, the doors and windows could not seal out that bitter wind. There was no snow. Just wind. The last big snow had melted the previous week. People began to talk about Spring.

"At seven-thirty in the morning, downstairs in the Basement, Alex Hartman, the janitor, was turning up the heat when he became a bit annoyed. He turned around and heard laughter by the stair well in the basement. He hollered out in a gruff voice with a slight Swiss accent, 'Who's doing that laughter?'

"Three little grade school girls came out of the shadows of the corridor laughing and giggling. 'We are sorry, Mister Hartman!' they said as they ascended the dry wooden stair case. 'We were only playing hide and seek!'

" 'You kidz don't come down here without permission! You could be hurt falling over something.'

"They ran on up the front stairs and disappeared in the corridors. Alex smiled to himself. He loved kids. Three of his own attended the school. As he stoked the furnace, he watched the pressure on the boiler. There was only one light bulb in the furnace room. He had electricity down there. Only a few rooms on lower levels of the building had electric lights. The rest of the rooms had oil lamps. For most of the rooms the main light came through the windows. On gray overcast days, the kids strained their eyes to read and write. That year, 350 children were enrolled. It was a small, crowded school. They came to learn, they came to grow up.

"In the basement, the furnace and the boilers created the steam that ran through the pipes and radiators in the nine rooms and two corridors. The steam moved from the basement all the way up to the third floor where there was an auditorium, which had recently been converted into a fifth grade classroom.

"Donny was a student there. In spite of his arrogance, he had many friends.

"There was always a problem with heating that building. When the third floor became warm, the rest of the room would be too hot. When the lower floors were pleasant, the third floor was too cold. In the winter, no one liked any temperature for too long. It was either too cold or too hot, but just right for about ten minutes between shifting temperatures. So students and teachers complained continuously.

"At eight thirty sharp, the children entered the school by the front and back doors. They came through a five-foot wide doorway, turned sharply to the right and ascended the five or six steps on narrow wooden staircases, and once at the landing, they turned to the left or right depending on which classroom they were in. Then they ascended five more steps. It was a cramped entrance. It was almost impossible for kids to go up and down at the same time. But no one thought it was dangerous. The building was originally designed to accommodate one hundred students, not three hundred and fifty. The fathers and mothers of Collin Wood did not have enough money for a new school, so they crammed all their kids into this small school and hoped for the best. On the first floor, there were four rooms for first and second graders. On the second, the third and fourth graders had four room. On the third floor, as I said before, there was a new classroom for fifth graders in a recently remodeled auditorium.

"The outer walls of the building were covered with brick and supported by steel beams. The frame and paneling inside was mostly wood, made from an oily type of yellow pine that had dried out over the long winters. The un-insulated steam pipes which ran behind the dry wooden walls and beams were hidden away out of sight, but they could be heard expanding and contracting all winter long. You gotta do what you gotta do sometimes. Those kids needed education. The families were not wealthy. This was the best school they could afford at the time.

"After eight thirty all the children were seated in nine classrooms where nine teaches calmed them down as the lessons began. Responsibilities. Accountabilities. Giggling. Laughing. Fighting and bickering. Kids are kids. After everyone had settled down, Alex went around carefully closing the front and rear doors. First, he closed the outside doors which stopped the big gusts of wind, then he turned around in the vestibule and closed the inside doors. The same routine. Day after day.

"The doors in that school always opened outward, but perhaps because it was dark in the vestibule, or maybe because Alex took care of the doors, many people thought the doors opened inward. Confusion is part of life. In a tragedy, confusion continues long after the event. When he had the front secured, he crossed the hallway at the top of the stairs, and he went over to the rear doors and did the same thing. Now the dry wooden building became warm as toast, and he descended to the basement and checked the furnace and the boiler. Everything looked fine. The Great Fire was about to begin.

"After checking everything, he walked around with a broom and dustpan and swept the leaves and mud out of the vestibules and corridors. At nine o'clock, he took a break. Some say he went home to his house which was a few doors down the Street. But if he did, he returned in fifteen minutes, and went down into the basement where he read the newspaper as he drank coffee and listened to the furnace. He always carried out his routines with care. Later, some would say in anguish that he also plotted a vicious, secret plot against all the children. But Alex never did that. He was a sober and serious man. Three of his own children attended the school. The children loved his smiling face and respected his gruff but friendly voice; and even though he scolded them sometimes, he cared for each one.

"At 9:40 A.M., Amanda Delaney excused herself from her classroom on the first floor. She entered the dim warm hallway, came quietly down the dark staircase in the front, turned at the tiny vestibule, and descended into the dim basement. As she descended the stairs, she felt the warm wooden walls. She could not see anyone at all. She hollered out to Mister Hartman and he answered her from his room by the furnace. She went to the girl's restroom, and then shortly returned to the stairway.

"Now this was the first sign of danger. As she came up the stairs, she saw a faint trail of smoke drifting from behind each wooden stair tread. It appeared to her as if some one stood there behind the stairs and smoked a cigar. As he smoked, he puffed the smoke through a thin crack in the oak panels. It was a most curious puff. For the more she stepped, the more it puffed. It frightened her because she had never seen it before. It was said that after she studied it for a moment, she said in a curiously loud voice, 'Mister Hartman, why is that smoke puffing through the wall?'

"And Hartman became concerned and asked, 'What did you say?'

"To which she exclaimed, 'I see smoke is puffing out of the stairs!'

"Alex came out of the boiler room, and he too saw the puffing smoke. Alarmed, he opened the door to the storage room under the stairs and discovered a wall of roaring flames. Instantly, he closed the door and charged up the stairwell, and ran into the first grade classroom and rang the fire alarm bell three times and hollered out, 'Fire! Fire!'

"Amanda ran back to her class and hollered, 'There's a fire down stairs,' as the bell rang.

"Now there was a fire drill routine in the school. Every kid knew how to line up and march out in an orderly manner. In those drills, they learned how to vacate the building calmly. Every child and teacher knew what to do. Drills were fun. They exited carefully by planned routes. The smaller kids on the first floor exited first, meanwhile the older kids on the second and third floors marched to the top of the stairways and waited in the hallway, and when instructions were given, they descended the stairways carefully and quickly, and walked through the vestibule doors without a hitch. 'A good drill only took ninety seconds,' the principal later reported.

"After ringing the bell three times, Alex ran to the double doors in the front of the building and pushed both set of doors wide open. Then he ran to the rear of the building and pushed the double set of doors open as wide as possible. Now it is believed the wind may have closed the rear door because someone found it shut. Soon the children on the first floor exited at the front door without a problem. They laughed and chattered.

They thought it was another fire drill until they came to the doorway and saw emerging flames and smoke.

"Meanwhile the kids at the top of the stairs hollered, 'False Alarm! False Alarm! It's only another drill!' But then it happened. The cold, swift wind swept through the corridors, fanning and enabling the fire. As the kids from the second floor came down they encountered other kids who raced up fleeing the flames in the doorways. Soon kids from the front door raced into a crowd of kids who tumbled into a pile at the rear door.

"Both doors were now blocked, and the big wind found its way through the back doors and rushed across the hallway over the children's head and roared out the front doors. More flames ascended rapidly, and the stairwells filled up with smoke and flames as if they were chimneys. Ninety seconds passed, and all the stairwells were engulfed with smoke as kids began falling everywhere. At the rear door stairwells, the bodies of children piled up. And then more kids came down from the third floor. Some still cried out, 'False alarm! False alarm! It's only another silly fire drill!'

"At the bottom of the stairs, where kids piled up on kids, some of the bolder boys leaped over the bodies of classmates to tumble out of the doors to safety. Once pinned down, the smaller, frailer children could not move. Suffocation was perhaps the best way to die on that day.

"Many children suffocated before their bodies burned. Adults, including Alex, ran to the doors and dragged children out of the vestibules and corridors. Some ran back into the building searching for others, a few of them never came out of the building.

"Some teachers, having discovered the flames at both doorways, guided as many children as they could to the northern end of the building where just outside the windows there was a fire escape. There, they began lowering children as fast as they could to the ground. Some kids fled back to their classrooms and broke the windows, and began leaping out of the building. Bernie Horowitz, a brilliant kid whose family I loved, leaped from the second floor, his hair and clothes burning. He never survived. Once their hair and clothing caught fire, there was not much time left. A few survived these perilous acts, but many who leaped while burning soon died. Some, including my son, broke open a window on the third floor and descended on the fire escape from the third floor.

"Fifteen minutes into the fire, more than half the students managed to get out of the building. But then ironically, a few of these reentered and perished as they searched for siblings and friends. With the windows open and the doors, the flames accelerated and engulfed the building. The horrible narrow stairwells soared with flames.

"One event was never forgotten by my son.

"High up in the auditorium, young Mike Wilson was trapped. He was a tough kid, a fighter. He propped a chair against a wall, then scaled the wall, then he jumped onto some panels that served as scenery for a play. Hand over hand, he boldly fought his way toward the fire escape at the north end of the building. As he came near the fire escape, a single hand reached out to him through an open window. Many on the ground watched him. They held their hands over their mouths and prayed. Mike clung by his fingers. Hand over hand he came across that long room, looking at that hand. Near the end, before he could reach out, surrounded by smoke and heat, he stopped looked at the hand, looked down below, lost his grip, plunged into the flames, and vanished.

"Shortly after that, the fire consumed the building as dark smoke billowed upward. Then , the first floor of the building plunged into the basement. Soon the remains of the second floor descended dragging with it the flaming auditorium. After two hours, all that stood was an empty shell of bricks and mortar. Of the 350 students, 168 died. Two teachers, one rescuer worker, and maybe some others were also consumed by the smoke and flames. Of the dead, many were never identified. Many survivors had severe burns. By 1:30 in the afternoon, the fire was completely out, and the living began to endure a life time of remorse, as Ash Wednesday March 4, 1908 lodged itself in human memory forever.

"I was burned on my arms. Donny got out unscathed. Right son?"

"Some might call it that way, dad. Some days I wished I died with my friends. This whole thing, this horrible fire, has made me hate God and man alike. But it's all nothing. Don't matter no more."

Ebb stopped talking.

The group stopped walking.

Silently they looked at the garden with its stairways and archways and a few green sprouts showing the early signs of spring . Then Uncle Henry said, "You have to understand. If you wish to make a tribute to those who passed on, you must first forgive yourself. No one should be blamed for what happened."

Ebb said, "All that was four years ago, as I recall. This is the first time I have returned to Collin Wood. Standing here, talking like this, I feel a strong desire to do something. I need to kneel down and pray. I think I know who I am now. I ain't no talker, but I'm a doer. I see this garden was built in memory of these kids. I want to build that cabinet in my shop in the memory of these kids. Yes! I can see now for the first time why that makes sense."

Ebb knelt down. Elmer bowed down beside him.

Everyone wept quietly – a kind of silence that was beyond speech. Except Donny who stared intently at the sky.

Finally Ebb stood up and said, "I couldn't talk about it, til now. Don't know why."

Elmer said, "Well all I got to say is the Church will help you anyway we can. Count us all in."

"I definitely will!" Ebb paused and then continued, "I can't cross this valley without my friends. I tried that, and fell like little Mike straight down into the flames of my own memory. As I look around, I see other people with great hearts have shown their generous love here. It's my turn to do something."

On the next day at 9:30 in the morning, the whole group came to the Memorial Garden for the annual service. They gathered in a circle and listened as the bells at St. Jerome's church tolled 175 times. Ebb looked around at the crowd. Many of the faces there were familiar. No one appeared to begrudge him or anyone for that matter. Some even greeted him and thanked him for being there. As he asked around, he soon learned that many people who lost children in the fire left for parts unknown and never came back. Some even left their clothes hanging in the closets and money in their bank accounts. It was a solemn memorial unlike anything he expected.

Chapter Fourteen

Jenny Joins a Church

Just as the Model T could not replace a good horse, so also a new faith springs in one way or another from some valued truth. And yet, in spite of the most obvious nature of this premise, contrary to all logic, a new faith may appear to open up the doorway to the heavens not only for the first time but often, as it seems, for the only time. For Jenny Collard, seeing her husband rise up with courage and defend his role in the school fire gave her a new religion. She decided to join The Community of One Church.

A week after the visit to the Garden, this joy of discovery spilled over into everything in her life. She bought new clothes. She cleaned and decorated her house. In this spirit, the women at the church invited her to take a special trip to Willowford. She was ready to become a new person wholly transformed from the inside out.

Of course, Ebb found all this disturbing. He was not so much surprised by her decision as he was shocked by the intensity of her expression. Whether he wanted it or not, she was about to be "wrapped in the arms of Jesus." For her it was a time to celebrate. But for him, the ordeal was a little more complicated.

Ebb loved his wife. He always saw within her a little girl on the brink of discovering a wonderland and somewhat shocked when she saw reality tarnish her expectations. He was a man with a harsh soul, hardened by harsh labor and meager financial rewards. He liked to think that his wife needed help that only he could provide, that he alone could revitalize that little girl within her without trampling her down at the same time. But this was hardly the case. So, when she decided to join the church, he felt it was because he had failed in his own mission to protect her, and this failure subverted his own pride in a manner he could neither express nor deny. All this came to the surface one Saturday morning in the summer of 1912 after they finished breakfast.

"You know, Ebb," she said cautiously as she cleaned up the dishes, "I've been to their services. It's just a small group. But on every first Sunday of the month, they gather for fasting and prayer, and the members stand up and thank each other for being supportive and helpful in times of trouble. There's no preacher, just a few elders who don't say much. The members share their deepest feelings. That's the whole service. I find it very meaningful."

"Hum? It's that Bible of theirs that throws me off. I mean the gold plates that disappeared as soon as they were found." Ebb sat in the kitchen where he poured himself another cup of coffee. He sensed this was going to be a delicate discussion. He did not share her enthusiasm, and yet he did not want to be overbearing. This was the new, kinder Ebb, the man whose deep wounds had been healed. Truth was he owed her an awesome moral debt, he just did not want her to know it.

"Well, Ebb, there's this elderly woman there, Sister Marley; she's read a lot of things and pondered all of it in her heart. She was once a Methodist. She told me everything in the The Book of Mormon can be traced back to the book of James in the regular Bible. She said she made a study of that and that's when she decided to join the Mormons. She said Joseph Smith grounded his faith in the book of James. Over and over, he talked about how faith has to be shown by good works done in a humble and quiet way. That without the deed, nothing much matters. Now that's what you find in James."

"Hum. James? Wasn't he supposed to be a brother to Jesus. I heard that somewhere once. Isn't that true?"

"Yes, that's what they say," she said, surprised to hear that her husband actually studied religion at all. "But James was modest. He never boasted about himself or his family. He was humble. But here's an important thing. When the Prophet was a young man, he was confused by all the different teachings of the Presbyterians, the Baptists, and the Methodist let alone the Catholics who worshiped their own Church's history. So he read in James where it says, If anyone lacks wisdom, then he should ask God directly, and God will give him the right answer once and for all."

"Hum? Ask God Himself? I guess you can't go wrong there," Ebb sipped his coffee and looked out the kitchen window at the deep woods where he himself sought spiritual refuge.

"Now Ebb, you startin' to sound like you're makin' fun of me," she said detecting a thin stream of sarcasm swelling up in her husband's mind.

"Jen, for four years, these folks been right helpful to us, but I can't quite accept them myself. Something spooky about a grown man who drops to his knees in the middle of the woods and outright sees Jesus and God standin' there in white robs talkin' to him at midday. Yet that's the kinda fella this *Prophet* was, as I understand it. I mean I'm sorry but that don't set right with me."

"Well, it sets right with me. All those other preachers done fell short of the truth in my opinion!"

"That's fine! That's fine, whatever helps you, helps me. Go ahead and join up."

"Well, I'm goin' to be baptized by them next week, and I want you to be there. And in a few days, Daisy Rodell, Alice, and I are goin into Willowford shopping together. I want a new dress for the occasion."

"That's fine. While you are there, can you pickup two pounds of eight penny nails at the hardware, for me?"

"Yes, just so long as you don't make fun of my conversion."

"Hum? Yep. Nary a word of evil will slip out of these lips. Nary a word. Hum."

"I heard a suspicious word in there somewhere!" she said as she cleaned the dishes in the sink.

"Hum! Nary a word!" he finally drew silent and went out to the barn to feed the horse.

That next week, she took that trip to town. It was yet another indication of spiritual healing, but something that happened there aroused Ebb's deep suspicion about "The Church."

Willowford was an old Victorian town that sat on a high ridge over the Chagrin Valley. The main street consisted of two blocks of buildings, two and three stories high with store fronts. Most of these were built from solid red brick. At the southern end of the town there was a V-shaped divide where the main road split into two roads. The eastern road followed the winding ridge above the valley, the western bent around a few curves, and then more or less ran straight into downtown Cleveland about sixteen miles due west. Most roads in the Western Reserve were nothing more than straight lines drawn on a map set down by Moses Cleveland and his surveying crew in the 1790's. The ridge road was different. It curved like a wiggling snake.

On that summer morning in 1912, some folks in Willowford were surprised to see three slightly hysterical woman in a black Model T Ford laughing and waving their hands as they swept around the curves of the Ridge Road. Daisy, Elmer's wife, sat nervously behind the wheel. Alice, the widow was beside her pointing at obstacles and bumps in the roadway, and Jenny was perched on the back seat where she held her hand over her mouth as she issued commands for Daisy to slow down even while she sped up to alarming speeds in excess of forty miles per hour! The three ladies were out having fun.

When they came to the V-shaped junction in the street, they slowed down to a crawl as Daisy carefully pulled the Model T Ford to a halt right near an enormous Civil War Cannon that was aimed straight down the center of Erie Street. Proudly anchored in a triangular garden, this cannon reminded everyone that, even though no battles were fought here, certain town members paid the last full measure of devotion as they fought for The Union. In those days, some of the persons listed on that monument were still remembered by the elderly residents.

When these three women stepped out on the sidewalk, they became the center of considerable gossip. For in those days, few women had the nerve to drive a horseless carriage straight into the center of a bustling town. And yet there they were chattering like birds at sunrise. They had mastered the secrets of driving an automobile; and so it was, they proudly walked the sidewalks exhilarated by their accomplishment.

"You know, Jenny," said Daisy, a thin and energetic woman with dark playful hair that extended down to her shoulders, "there are so many new inventions these days. I mean, just the other day Elmer showed me a new kind of washing machine that squeezed the water out of your clothes.

Then he had a new kind of gasoline engine that he said he could connect to the washer so that you did not have to crank it by hand. Now he's talking about getting a telephone in the house no less, and believe it or not, why last month, he bought me a new kind of cabinet that you put right in the kitchen. It has everything you need, to make bread and pies and cakes, right at your finger tips, including, mind you, a built in flour sifter! Could you imagine that? There should be a demonstration of one around here today."

"A cabinet," said Jenny who was dressed in a spotless pink dress with her hair propped up above her ears. She pressed her hair back while she glanced at her reflection in a window. "Why my Ebb built me a handmade baker's cabinet years ago. It works just fine. Buy a cabinet! Why Ebb would have a fit if I did that!"

"But listen. Just wait 'til you see this one. They're supposed to have a demonstration somewhere around here. It has a sifter, a sugar bin, a spice rack, a big drawer for pots and pans, and a small one for utensils. Mary Belle has one, and she said she sits *down* to work. Imagine that. She sits down to work! No running around in circles. She just sits down to work! Ha! Ha! Ha! I just have to see where that demonstration man will be today! I want to sit down to work!"

"Well," Jenny said, "I can most likely skip that."

"Oh, Jenny, I've seen that thing Ebb built for you," said Alice, a stocky woman with a stiff lower lip and lots of wrinkles from hoeing her garden in the sun. "I mean its nice and all, but it doesn't even come close to one of these new models. Why I have one myself, and look here I have an ad from the paper. It says right here it only costs $25.00, and better yet, you can buy it on the installment plan for $5.00 a month, and they even give you free glassware."

"For goodness sake, look at that! A Hoosier Cabinet? What's a Hoosier anyway?" asked Jenny.

Daisy stopped and looked around, "They had a man in town two weeks ago selling these at the furniture store. Look over there! I believe that's him in that place right over there. That man came here all the way from Indiana. Hoosiers always come from Indiana for some reason. Let's go see if he will be here today."

Along side the Model T Ford, the Hoosier cabinet was a major invention of the early twentieth century. Between 1910 and 1933, millions of these stand-alone kitchen cabinets were manufactured mostly in Indiana and distributed around the country. They were mass-produced usually out of oak and had thin plywood panels and narrow posts mounted on casters. Women loved them. But for certain cabinetmakers of the old school, such as Ebb, they were an abomination.

The ladies chattered as they walked among the horse drawn wagons and the sputtering automobiles and the men and women dressed up in the latest and brightest clothes and some children running after their pet dog who broke free from his leash. For Jenny mingling with the crowds filled her with an excitement she had not known since they left old Collin Wood. She felt as if the little girl within her was about to skip rope at a faster and faster pace as she giggled and counted her hops. She felt like singing "One Mississippi! Two Mississippi!" There were many reasons for her rebirth. But the primary one was a feeling that God himself smiled on her as He looked down from His heavenly throne saying. "One Mississippi! Two Mississippi! Three Mississippi!"

"There, it's right there!" said Daisy as she turned about quickly and pointed at a sign. "There's his sign right across the street. Let's see what it says!" All three jumped off the side walk and laughed as they darted in front of a car that blew its "Oogah" horn as it weaved to avoid them. They circled around a sign in the store window.

TODOY ONLY

TODAY ONLY
Denny The Hoosier Man will demonstrate
The latest time and laboring kitchen cabinet
Here in Adam's furniture store.
At One O'clock sharp
Special Gifts for all who place orders

"We have two hours to wait," said Alice, "let's get a lunch and go up by the park. That is, unless you want to continue shopping?"

"I need to get some nails and my new dress," said Jenny as she looked back at the hardware store.

"I need to stop at that new dress shop myself," said Daisy.

So they decided to meet at the park in one hour and then have lunch and return here together for the demonstration. So they dispersed.

When they returned in about two hours, Jenny stepped reluctantly into the store behind the others. She had no intention of buying anything. A group of women had already gathered in front of three cabinets. They talked to a handsome young man who wore a straw hat and swung a long thin cane. He sported a bright bow tie and a huge smile, and on a long chain, he had a gold pocket watch about the size of a baby's fist. He talked as fast as a boiling steam kettle and looked at the watch repeatedly.

"Ladies and gentlemen, it's now one o'clock and I have to catch a train to Buffalo at five. So if you would, please find a chair, so we can begin. There are extra folding chairs by the wall there if we need more."

The excited trio found a place in the fourth row where Jenny could see by looking around a woman's broad hat with a red ribbon on it. She felt the energy in that room as the man rattled on like a machine.

"How many people here today have heard the words, 'Efficient Time Management'?"

Two or three people shyly raised their hands. He thanked them and went onto explain a little history of the latest domestic kitchen science studies and then quickly moved on to the cabinets. "Now over here, ladies and gentlemen, I have a brand new, fully-equipped Hoosier Model 162. If you will notice, a solid easily cleaned porcelain counter top. Imagine yourself rolling your dough over that non sticking surface. Now to the right here, you find a flour sifting bin so large it will contain enough flour for one month. To get it out, no problem, just turn this little handle. No mess. No heavy sack to lift. Just turn the handle. The mixing bowl is stored right on this shelf." He went on to quickly demonstrate most of the forty "work reducing features" and the drawers and shelves designed to hold four hundred work utensils "at your finger tips."

Jenny leaned over and nudged Alice with her elbow, "My! That man talks fast!"

"He's a salesman all right."

"Are you ready to make cake ladies? Feast your eyes on these shelves. *You* have large bowls, medium bowls, small bowls. Spatula, spoons, and a a handy mixer. And if that's not enough, look here at *your* food storage bin sealed so no nocturnal visitors can get at your cake or bread. Now let me open this sliding panel and voila! Here's *your* spice jar canister wheel with eight of *your* favorite spices.

"Now if I may, I would like to ask one lady to come forward. Let's see. How about the fine young woman peeking around the corner in the fourth row there. What's your name, mam?"

"Who me? Jenny. Jenny Collard."

"Yes Jenny! Lovely name! Thank you! Come right on down! Sweet name. Had an aunt called Jennifer when I was a child. She had seven children. Why she ran a marathon every time she served a meal. Poor soul died before she was fifty. Now Jenny, I want you to sit right here on the stool. That's right. Just relax. No more running a marathon. Reach over there and turn the sifter. That's right. Now reach down there and pick up that big bowl and place it on the top. Now open that drawer and take out the rolling pin. Now reach in there and turn the spice jars and remove the cinnamon. Thank you. Ladies and Gentlemen, I asked Jenny to do this because she is petite. Now she just performed five basic chores involved in baking. Have you seen her yet stand on her feet? Or walk across a room? Or move off of that stool? Not once!"

Jenny looked briefly around at the group of fifty or sixty women whose eyes strained as they focused on Denny O'Toole. Alice waved and smiled. Jenny blushed. Denny glanced at her briefly and winked. "Ladies, let me ask you a question. Wouldn't it be fun to take a leisurely walk through the park with your husband and kids on a Saturday afternoon? Wouldn't that be more fun than working yourself to exhaustion in a sweltering kitchen. Why of course it would! Throw off those shackles. The Hoosier manufacturing company has come to deliver you from the drudgery. Now before I start taking your orders, there's a couple of things I want to tell you about our simple payment plans. But first, let us all give Jenny a round of applause. Thank you, you may return."

As she stood up, Denny extended his finger tips and touched her hand briefly. Suddenly, she felt like Cinderella dancing in a ballroom. Her whole world transformed around her. Before she got to her seat, she already decided. She did not know why. It was just "another part of God's eternal plan." Ebb's old handmade Baker's cabinet would have to go out to that silly stable, and this new cabinet was about to be put in its place. She just had to buy a Hoosier today.

When they returned to the car that afternoon, Jenny turned pale for a moment. The euphoria of the sale had worn off. She took her place in the back seat and said, "Ebb's going to be mad at me!"

"Why?" said Daisy as Alice cranked the engine. "All you did was make life more comfortable for yourself, and for him too. Think of it. Better yet, don't think of it. When they bring that cabinet out tomorrow, we'll both come over, set it up, and bake a pie. What's Ebb's favorite pie?"

"Apple."

"All right. I have some really sweet canned apples. I'm going to bring them over when we come. We're going to give that man a surprise. Soon you will make breads, cakes, apple pies, and in less time and with less effort. Yes don't think about it, just do it to it. Right Alice?"

"Yes indeed," she said as she climbed and secured the door. "We are all Sisters now. Members of the Community of One. And we are going to take care of you and your family. And listen to this, I've talked to the women's group and they already decided. Now that we know you want it, here's the surprise. We will buy this cabinet for you, and you don't owe us one cent."

"Oh, my goodness! You don't have to do that?" said Jenny as she took a deep breath.

"We want to do it," said Daisy as she turned the car around in the street and headed out of town on the Ridge Road at top speed. "I don't want to hear another word about that. It's yours."

"My husbands a cabinetmaker, and you folks bought me a factory made cabinet!" said Jenny.

"Listen to her!" said Alice, and they all laughed so hard they almost cried.

In the evening on the next day, Ebb came home late riding his wagon with Finny in the harness. They moved slowly after a long hard day at the Garfield House called Lawnfield. He was impressed by a large desk there called a Wooten. It was the center piece in the Library in that big mansion. Just the sight of it inspired him. His heart felt strangely warmed as he thought of the idea of building something complicated and beautiful like that desk, but he just could never find the time and energy. He had to make a living, and that meant humbling himself in service to others. He was thankful that he had a roof over his head and a well flowing with water, a small garden, a few good places to hunt and fish, a young son who still needed him, and his devoted wife. He counted his blessings one by one as he unhitched old Finny and led him into the stall in the barn and locked the door.

When he finally entered the house, he was met with a wife whose clothes and hands and hair were covered with white flour. There on the counter were three apple pies still warm from the oven, and five loaves of bread not yet baked as they rose slowly in metal bread pans. And there, where his clumsy old cabinet once stood was the New Hoosier cabinet all a glow with a golden oak finish. Every door, every drawer, every cranny was wide open, and the insides were lined with every utensil his wife ever had. All this was within reach from a stool which stood next to the porcelain top.

"Isn't it beautiful!" said Jenny as she gave him a big hug putting flour marks all over his shirt.

"What in tarnation is goin' on now? You and those women from the church have been up to something, haven't you?"

"We sure have! Ebb I've been havin' so much fun baking with this new Hoosier cabinet. It's just so easy. Daisy, Alice, and the church women bought it yesterday, and they came over and set it up today. Look I even got a free cookbook with it. And here, just for you, a piece of my first apple pie that I put together in just a few minutes right here on the porcelain counter."

Now what happened at that moment was the culmination of many years of inscrutable agony. The poor man's sustained anger at himself had only begun to find relief, when suddenly the props slid out from under his feet. He set his lunch pail down by the sink. He walked over and looked at the cabinet, and felt the door with his finger tips.

"How could such a cheap plywood cabinet bring so much joy to one person?" he asked, puzzled as deep fears welled up within him.

"Because it works easy," she said.

In that moment, he started to laugh like never before.

He realized there was something special about those simple people. They moved so swiftly and quietly right into the center of his home. He laughed more as he ate his apple pie and studied that cabinet.

He had his doubts – deep doubts about many things. But there was no doubt here. It hit him like a kick from a mule:

"Plywood! I been done in by *plywood*!"

Chapter Fifteen

Peculiar Signs of the End

Ebb had his doubts about the *modern* world. These doubts were actually anchored much deeper than most people thought. He had a faith which he seldom shared with anyone, perhaps because he did not understand it himself.

Ebb believed in a few notions handed down by his father, who was a semi-illiterate carpenter by trade. He kept these notions close to his heart. These notions were recorded in a peculiar Bible commentary published in London first in the 1890's and periodically revived by a maker of religious tracts. The original book was entitled, "Peculiar Signs of the End of the World" and was based on someone's reading of Matthew 24. Ebb had the book for years.

Behind these "peculiar signs", there was a premise that held that a sudden abundance of knowledge of the natural world and a seeming mastering over nature through advanced technology would indicate the encroaching end of the world. This premise was supported by a list of examples that alarmed many true believers in the apocalypse. The authors of "Peculiar Signs" not only published a watch list of these deviant inventions of modern technology, but periodically made additions and encouraged true believers to do the same.

Ebb opened this book only on special, frightening occasions. That evening was one such occasion. In his living room by an oil lamp, he perused it with tears of joy and sorrow. To this sacred list of inventions – signs of the imminent end of the world – he added his own along with a brief commentary, for there was a kernel of wisdom with each item:

The Balloon, 1798, it could easily burst.

The Gas Light, 1798, it could ignite a building.

The Cast Iron Plow, 1800, it could not be quickly repaired.

The Steam Powered Boat, 1807, it could explode and sink

The Steam Powered Printing Press, 1811, it could proliferate cheap books

The Revolver Pistol, 1818, a tool for thieves

The Railroad Car, 1825, it could derail easily

Photography, 1839, it could encourage vanity and pornography

Sewing Machine, 1846, it could injure a woman's hands

The Monitor War Ship, 1862, it could sink

The Typewriter, 1868, it could discourage good handwriting

The Phonograph, 1877, it could never produce an authentic sound

The Electric Railway, 1879, it could run over children and pets

Wireless Telegraphy, 1895, it could easily fail in a natural disaster

The Motion Picture, 1895, it lent itself to vanity

The Aeroplane, 1903, clearly designed for disaster

To these Ebb added his own observations in the margin, even adding one more that night:

A door that opened outward, 1907, could be broken by high wind

A door that opened inward, 1908, it could become a fire trap

The Model T Ford, 1908, you would always need a good horse

Plywood, 1912, more glue than wood

All of these inventions, and there were many more, occurred after 1798, which according to this book was some sort of watershed year in the French Revolution. Prior to that date, the conveniences and tools of all mankind remained pretty much the same since the time of Solomon's temple roughly 3000 years ago. These peculiar signs of the end of the world were not merely a secret source of private dread, but also a source for deep personal inspiration. They challenged the true believer to act now in the name of enduring quality.

Out in the stable, behind his house, for years he had been building benches and clamps and tools for his own work shop; and now an "apostate" cabinet had invaded the sanctuary of his kitchen. This was a sign of something. The hour had come and now was here for him to act. The devil was here, but what should he do? The Hoosier looked so nice.

Sitting there with his own Bible, he resolved once more to build his cabinet the classic way. Solid wood, with mortise and tenon joints, and hand-cut dovetails. It would be much better than that *plywood* thing.

The whole world was changing. It was like a balloon that could burst. He could see how that Hoosier served her needs now. But the overall structure just made him nervous. Moreover, it aroused fears and suspicion about the end of the world. But he did not want to say anything at this time. Jenny was too happy. When it broke like a gas balloon, as he knew it would, his vision would furnish a better version of the same thing. For now, her being happy gave him a window of opportunity.

After about twenty minutes of euphoria, Jenny came into the room and put her hand on his shoulder. She was a little apprehensive about her impulsive decision and her mysterious husband. She said, "Ebb, are you all right? You're acting strange."

"Jen," he said as he slid his weird book on "Peculiar Signs" into its special drawer. "I'm overjoyed because I have not seen you so happy in years. I will come to your baptism this Saturday, and to the church on Sunday. I have a good job going now with the Garfield family. Their father was a President of the United States, you know. I'm a lucky man. Who knows? I may build them that cabinet in the stable and sell it to them for good money. They already have an amazing desk there in the library. A little different than mine. If I could get them interested like I did with Feargus, maybe I could make some extra money and get us an automobile. Then, I could break loose!"

"Well, that project seems to take a long time. Not days, not months, but years. I don't understand why."

"It's hand selected wood, and it's hand carved, that's why. It's the old way. The ancient way. It endures longer," he said

"I see," she said quietly knowing what it meant to him. "Someday, you'll find time for it."

"Oh, I can see how you will enjoy that thing you bought. It looks nice," he said as he secretly pondered spending more time in his shop. "By the way, where is Donny?"

"Oh, you know those boys. They have a campsite on the river. Friends from the church keep an eye on them."

"I've neglected that boy. Seems to have never learned how to be responsible for himself."

"He comes by and gets food in the afternoons and takes off."

"Well, summer's comin', and they're country boys," he said. "I'd ask him to help me, but I know the answer. There is only one kid who will come here and help me on my special project and that's Billy Hasseler, as true a Saint as there ever was."

"His mom and Daisy were here all day."

"That's amazing!" said Ebb as he gently invited his wife to sit on his lap. "The end of the world as we know it may not be so bad after all. It could be the beginning of something better."

"What on earth are you talking about?" she asked.

"Nothing important," he said. He did not want a balloon to burst in his house that night.

That Saturday morning, a fair-sized crowd gathered on the edge of the River just beyond the store. The group sang a few hymns and offered up prayers, and then Abner Steele walked with Jenny into the center of the river. He said her full name and gave her a blessing, and then gently tilted her backward until she was fully submerged; and then just as gently, he helped her rise up where she paused for a moment, brushed her hair back, and smiled as she saw her husband and son standing on the shore.

Jenny's baptism was part of a tradition. Ancient. Unforgettable. A miraculous act of cleansing and rebirth. Afterwards, they went up to the Temple for a celebration dinner with prayers and testimonies. Ebb and Donny met the whole congregation. Of course, they knew almost everyone; but now, everything was different. His wife was a member. At the dinner, Elmer and his friend Abner, who ran the water driven Mill, approached Ebb in private.

"Ebb," said Elmer. "We've talked about it for years, and now we are going to do something about it. We, every person here today, are going to help you build that cabinet. We have a plan put together. We are going to plow and plant crops on that ten acre field of yours, and give you the biggest share of the produce and profit so you can find time to build that cabinet in your shop this coming winter. We will do all this out of love."

"But?" said Ebb.

"No buts. I was there at the Memorial Garden on my knees beside you when God told me to do this. There is a reason beyond my understanding. God wants that cabinet built, that's all I know."

It was a moment, he could never forget. All the pieces of his shattered soul suddenly fit back together as if they had never been broken. It was his dream as a kid, and he was going to complete it for the sake of those kids in that school.

Chapter Sixteen

The Harvesters Arrive

Early in the morning on September 24, 1912, Ebb saw a man in prayer. It happened this way.

He came out of his barn shortly after sunrise and saw Elmer driving out to the Collard farm on a steam-powered tractor. The red ball of the sun had just begun to break out behind the violet and maroon clouds gathered over the eastern horizon. The last stars, save Venus, had faded only minutes ago. The robins and wrens had ceased their lively, early chatter and were darting about the sky.

The plan was all but complete.

They prayed and listened to God, and then they acted. It was God's way, not theirs. In mid June, they plowed his ten acre field. Then in late June they planted tomatoes, corn, and a two acres of wheat. It was Ebb's farm land, but they worked it for him their way. Their only payment was a share of produce. But when they were done, he would be stock-piled with food and some cash for the winter. There would be no excuse now. These folks did this because they wanted to see the cabinet. Now he had the time to work, and somehow, he had to show them what he intended to do from the depth of his soul.

So on that morning as the tractor rolled carefully over the rough road under its own power at a maximum speed of about five miles per hour, he watched, astonished by what they were doing. It crept along like a green dinosaur grazing on the land. Except for the swishing and hissing of its valves, it made almost no noise. From the ground up to the canopy, it was every bit of ten foot tall, and the length of it about fifteen foot. Among the numerous attachments, nothing was as impressive as the big drive wheel, about four foot in diameter, that clung high up on the hip; once engaged, this wheel would pull the long six inch wide leather belt that would in turn drive the threshing machine.

Every little stone or chuck hole rocked the giant gently, but it seemed almost nothing could stop the slow advance of this ponderous Behemoth. Elmer guided it carefully by a steering wheel and a few levers, but the main problem of the steam tractor was the fire under the boiler. The clinkers, which were found amid the hot coals on the grid beneath the main boiler, were the most dangerous thing about the steam tractor. If one or two clinkers, which were made of stone or gravel, formed on the grid, a cool spot might form in the fire, and this could cause uneven heat to transfer to the walls of the boiler. Uneven heat could force a weld or a bolted seam to burst, and when that happened, the entire boiler could blow up in a matter of seconds. Some tractors, weighing over a ton, were known to blow up and rise twenty or more feet in the air, killing and injuring workers and bystanders. So every few minutes, Elmer opened the furnace door and examined the coals and with long tongs, he pulled out anything that even looked like a clinker, then he closed the door quickly. He took no chances.

Ebb stood frozen in the pathway in front of his barn for a moment. He watched as Elmer strained his eyes and looked forward and behind him at the road. He knew that he was listening and feeling every vibration of the steam boiler and the gears. He recognized that absolutely sober and stern look on his face. Elmer guided that tractor with his soul as the man prayed for maximum wisdom as he piloted this beautiful yet dangerous machine. At a precise point, Elmer turned off the road and drove it up along the edge of the wheat field, where he stopped it on level ground. There he stoked the fire and looked again for clinkers.

Donny had come out of the barn by then. He held a pitchfork in his hand as he stood slightly behind his father. "She's a beauty," he said.

Ebb was so rapt by the scene, he did not know his son was behind him. He glanced back and said, "Yep, but there's something different about the prayers of that Mormon. Could you see it in his face?"

"I know what you mean, pa. Can't put it in words."

"Neither can I, son. Just something different."

About a half hour after the tractor, the harvest team arrived. There must have been thirty people. They came in wagons and automobiles. They brought three wagons for hauling off chaff, one for the grain, and the thrasher itself. The crew were mostly Mormons, and some had been working together for years so they knew what was expected of them. On this field today, all would be paid in small sacks of flour to be furnished after the process was over. This was because there was no cash available from the Collard family. Before proceeding Abner Steele summoned everyone to a high spot on the hill near to the steam tractor. They all stood in a circle. Hatless, they bowed their heads in prayer. Abner spoke in a loud voice:

"Our Heavenly Father, we thank thee for your bounteous gifts poured out from the land. We thank you for generous rain from clouds and heavenly sunlight from beyond this world. Without these, there is no life. We come here today not to help one man and his family prepare for a special task assigned for them to the Glory of God, but for all of us. We leave our work in your hands, and now we beseech you, keep us safe as we labor. Amen."

After the prayer, which Ebb did not quite understand, the work began. It lasted for three days. Each noon, a group of woman came with a wagon load of food served in makeshift camp right in front of the farm house. That was the first time they grew wheat in that field. For many years, it was somtimes a corn or hay field, or more often nothing but pasture.

Around one o'clock, after the harvesters had their lunch and returned to the field to work, Abner and Elmer came down to where Jenny and Ebb helped the ladies reload their wagons. They packed up their dishes, silverware, table clothes, and the remaining food into baskets and departed for their homes. After the last garrulous group left, Ebb, Jenny, Abner, Elmer, and Donny sat down for few moments under a giant red oak that must have been two hundred years old. It was shady there and the five of them sat in a half circle so they could keep an eye on the workers.

As expected, the conversation turned to the religion; but what was unexpected was that Ebb's private secret personal dream of building a special cabinet right here in the wilderness, suddenly moved to the forefront.

Abner was a balding man with a broad forehead and stout shoulders.

He had a quick and nimble tongue, and thick, strong fingers characteristic of those who did hard labor. When young, he was quite assertive and combative, but he had mellowed over the years. He ran a sawmill on the Chagrin, and was an elder in the church. His grand father brought the gears and designs for a woolen mill from Leeds, England in the 1820's. It was quite an advanced wheel in its day, since it was only about ten feet in diameter, and it ran swiftly inside a narrow and fast sleuth. When the Mormons came in the1830's, his grandfather at first refused to join them, but gradually after weighing the alternatives, he was baptized along with his whole family. When the banks failed in 1838, his father kept his property with the aid of a "rich uncle," and decided not to leave for Missouri with the main group. For three generations, the Steele family ran the mill. For many decades, it was a woolen mill, producing cloth and winter clothing. When wool making became less profitable and the owners of large country estates began building fashionable homes, they converted the old mill to a saw mill, and did well. Although a Mormon, many of his beliefs were forged in the refiners fire of a rigorous life. They were just a little different from everyone else.

After discussing the harvest project briefly, the conversation turned to woodworking.

Elmer said, "You know, Ebb, I'm beginning to think this plan is working out. I think you will find time to work that project you have back there in the stable. Are you still interested?"

"Yeah, it's there all right, been there for years, but I've always been tied up with other things."

"You mean life gets in the way! That's what you're talking about," said Abner. "I know that problem. Many of my dream projects never got off the shelf because life gets in the way!"

"But this one's different though," Elmer said. "Ebb feels a call from God. Isn't that so? I mean remember when we talked about that atonement and all that with Henry last spring."

Ebb began rubbing his hands as he often did when he became nervous. "Years ago, people turned on me. They said I deliberating hurt a lot of kids. Sure, I made some mistakes. But nothing like what those folks said ever happened. I find it hard to forgive them. Working on fine woodworking helps me say something. It's like a prayer. You can't make any money doing carving and such. Not around here anyway. It's a spiritual thing, if you know what I mean."

Abner leaned forward and looked at Ebb directly, "I know what you mean. There's only one solution to something like that. You have to take it to God in prayer. You understand, my friend, that is one of the reasons these harvesters are here working. If I may be so bold for a moment. When The Prophet translated the The Book of Mormon, he spent three years. He lived in a log cabin with a young restless wife. The community in general thought he was a fool. But he prayed. He even wrote down his prayers in a book. He took the whole matter to God, and God said expect neither money nor fame, and you will get something better than both. You will build a great church. And he did. Cost him his life, but he did it. The man never had any money, but he had something greater than that. He had faith. My grandfather knew the man quite well. "

"What did he pray for?" Ebb asked.

"Purity of heart. Yep, that was The Prophet. He had a vision of a restored church rebuilt right in the home land of the Nephites, an ancient community. He did not want to do this for money or power, only to restore the lost kingdom of God that Jesus promised to all mankind. Yep, just an ordinary man, kinda had a limp when he walked. He prayed everyday and meditated on his writings for hours. Listening, always listening for messages from God."

"Hum," said Ebb, "I'm no preacher. No prophet. Come on back and see this project. Maybe you can see what I have in mind."

"Let's go," said Elmer. "The harvesters can take care of themselves for a while."

So they went, all four of them, Jenny and Ebb holding hands. As they walked, Ebb explained some things about the old horse farm that once was back here during the days after the Civil War. It was a decent place, had about twenty horses here. The stable was thirty foot long and twenty foot wide, with plenty of windows and a high ceiling. Years ago, Ebb tore down the stalls and used the lumber to make a wooden floor that was held up by locust post buried in the ground. Along the walls, he hung some of his tools, and then by a long window in the northern light, he had his big handmade bench with vices on both ends. But on this day, as he opened the door, it was clear that something had gone wrong. The place was a mess.

To get to the bench, he had to push his way through piles of junk. Once he cleared a path, which took a few minutes, he came to the bench and pulled up that dusty old tool chest, the same one he showed Feargus years ago. He said, " This chest belonged to my great grandfather. He built cabinets back in Connecticut before the Revolutionary War. He probably came from England as a servant. Our family never had much money. When I was still a child, my grandfather gave me this tool box. He said something I have always believed. He said that in every tree you can find the hand print of God. He always said cut your boards square and flat and smooth, but also at an angle so that you can see the finest patterns in the grain. He said if you do it right, you can see the heart of Jesus, just as if He rose again. It was some sort of creed, handed down for centuries. I mean the grain in the wood and the marks on your hands spring from the same source, God."

Abner looked with great deal of concern. "If I might suggest something, you need to organize this place just a tad."

"Yeah we will get to that. On this sheet here, you see the drawing he made centuries ago."

Old Abner moved in close and tilted the drawing so the window light illumined them. "Son," he said in a firm voice, "I've heard talk of this project for a long time actually. Kids and others come around and talk about it. This is a beautiful idea. But you need some serious help. Somebody has got to clean up all this junk." He set the drawing down and put his hands behind his back for moment. "What does that word mean to you? That word right there: *Koladari*."

"Eh? Don't know exactly. Some say it's an ancient source for my family name. Means something like the handprint of God. God's handprint is found everywhere."

"I see. Now I'm right curious about this project! You see, that word means something else to me. Okay, Now, Ebb Collard, I'm going to make you an offer right here and now. I can see this will take some work. I will do this, in part because your wife is a member of the church, but as I see it, this project is about you and your soul. The harvesters are here to gather your grain, sell it, and buy you time to complete this project. If you want, we will, God willing, help you complete this before December. But there are a few rules. First, we will help you in any way we can, but you cannot do this for money. You have to do this for the love of doing it."

"Not money?" Ebb said slightly startled.

"We won't help you, if you do it for money. Makes sense, doesn't it? No money! I'm not sure if you understand why. It has nothing to do with the time that we will take. It has everything to do with the prayers you will offer to God while you do this. Are you willing to do it for nothing? Then there's the bigger question. Are you willing to do it for God?"

"I'm not too sure what you mean," Ebb asked as he looked askance at the old man.

"Do you want to be absolutely sure?"

"I believe so."

"Then you need a *discernment blessing*, I am an elder of the Church. I can give you that."

"What does that mean?"

"If God wants you to do this, then you must do it. If He doesn't, you probably will never do it. What you need to know is what God wants you to do. I cannot determine that for you. I can only give you a discernment blessing. You can sit here on this stool, and I will place my hands on your head, and I will pray for you. No one else needs to know anything about this. Just the people here now."

"It sounds like something weird or spooky to me," said Ebb.

"Nothing of the kind!" said Abner. "We, members of the church, do this all the time. It's an ancient ritual."

"But I'm not a Mormon."

"Doesn't matter. I would like to do this for anyone long as he or she had a willing heart. Catholic, Protestant, Jew, anyone. Even Muslim or a Buddhist. We do it all the time."

"Well, let's get it done and see what happens."

"Sit here. What is your full name?"

"Ebeneezer Collard." Ebb set down facing the northern window that he loved.

Abner placed his warm hands firmly on Ebb's head. The old man spoke in a firm yet positive voice.

"Father in heaven we lift up before you Ebeneezer Collard, a person of your creation. A member of your Holy Kingdom. We ask in humility on his behalf that you will guide and help him with your unwavering charity. Show him what he must to do to find purity of heart. Help and guide him as he works to express his love for You. Open up his heart and let him express himself in a way he never has in his entire life. As he works in this beloved workshop, open his mind to your purposes in having him do this; and if it be not your purpose to have him do this, guide him as he reconciles all the perplexities of those dreams that are never done. Teach this fine man to listen to the intent of his own soul, which will be your intent when his heart is pure. We ask this in the name Jesus Christ. Amen."

Ebb remained seated with his head bowed. He felt a little dizzy. Finally, he stood up and shook the hands of his friends. "Thank you, I will continue saying that same prayer. Yes, indeed. I will remember this moment. Thank you."

"God will guide you, but right now let's haul some of this useless stuff over to your hay barn. If you ever need someone to help you on this project, never hesitate to call on me night or day. I too am a cabinetmaker and a millwright, and I want to see this project completed before Christmas time. Yes, I want to be there to celebrate the Atonement Blessing of Ebb Collard." And with that, he picked up the gasoline engine and the broken wheel and hauled them out to the barn without even asking permission.

Elmer stayed for a moment, and shook Ebb's hand, and said, "We are all with you," and he picked up the fishing gear and other clutter and hauled it out. "This gonna be a fine workshop, starting right now!" he said.

Ebb looked at Jenny and Donny and shook his head. "Well, we got friends."

Donny grabbed a broken plow, but he shook his head and said little, "Don't make sense," he mumbled. "None of us did nothing wrong ever. Never in fact! We don't need no forgiveness?"

"That's all right, son," Ebb said as he pushed a wheel barrow full of farm tools out the door. "This is not about right and wrong, it's about something else."

"What's it about?"

"After centuries of being buried, the Koladari is coming to life."

The men worked for about an hour. After they left, Ebb looked at Jenny. He hugged her and said, "Right now, I think I'm going to do this. But I don't exactly know what just happened here. Can you figure it out?"

"Ebb, they are just plain folks. They love you because they all have their own frustrated dreams, just like everyone else, and they want to be your friend. They want to see you fulfill your dreams. They are just plain, humble people. Maybe this is what you need to understand."

For Ebb the problem he saw for that moment and for many months to follow, was he felt, the oldest perplexity of mankind, the need for money. The old man's words struck his soul like a lightening bolt. "You cannot do this for money." That was the very reason that kept him from doing it all along! He always felt he could never make money on such a tedious project. That's why he never worked on it. So then, what did the man mean with the *Discernment Blessing*?

Slowly, he began to *discern* what his grandfather meant by the hand print of God. It was not just the beauty of wood and carvings, but the beauty of life itself as it permeated creation and manifested itself through wood, perhaps the hardest living substance. That beauty surrounded us everywhere, and we knew it not. He saw that by making this cabinet for no money, he could fulfill a deep yearning in his soul, and send a message to many others. He could express his humble gratitude to the Creator of the world. This deeply motivated him. Yet in some ways, he felt it was too deep for a humble craftsman. He realized what he was learning: that he needed the whole community, the harvesters, the women who brought lunch, and the elders who guided them all, and yes, even his wife's support.

Through prayers and prayers alone, could he fulfill not only a childhood dream, but also an atonement – a setting of things right between himself and God? If so, deep inside he felt with some fear that he just might become a *true Believer*.

But Abner mentioned nothing about that. He didn't have to.

Outside, up the hill, one more important private conversation took place. When Elmer came up there, Abner took him aside from the harvesters and asked, "How well do you know this man?"

"Oh, pretty well. We camped and fished and did a few odd jobs. Why do you ask?"

"It's very simple. We are in the process of standing him face to face with God. Also, his wife, and the son. Some people do crazy things when that happens. That boy, Donny, it seems he's runnin' from himself most of the time. He has a peculiar way of rollin' his head back and lookin' at the ceiling. It's an angry look comes across him when he does that. You told me yourself, he ain't all there."

"He's a wild one all right."

"The father too. You never know what drives a person like him. Hell fire and rage and all sorts of bad memories. Revenge against someone else, that's another thing. You just never know how fast that kettle's boilin' within someone like that. Just keep an eye on them. We have to come back from time to time just to keep things runnin' steady."

"They'll be all right," said Elmer.

"Don't be too sure! You never known what happens when a Godless man confronts his own heart."

Chapter Seventeen

The Turning Mill Wheel

⧖

Steele's Mill, like many other villages, was a community built around a mill. A good mill changed not only the course of a river, but the course of history. Towns emerged out of the wilderness as communities flourished. Often, after the mill shut down, the town remained.

Around 1800, when the first waves of pioneers with land grants made their way into the Western Reserve, they usually came in covered wagons and had to cut their own roads. They often followed trails left by trappers, natives, as well as wild animals. Once they settled on their acres, they used the canvas on the wagon to erect a tent. They might spend five to ten years, summer and winter, in that tent, felling trees to build their first cabin and open up land for a farm.

During those harsh times, they established a kinship with the land and its people. Once the primitive villages and towns were established, it did not take long for skilled people to build the water powered mills. After they were up and running, the rugged pioneers could build farm houses, grind grain, and process wool. The mill brought civilization. Often, the towns that grew up around the mills were named for the mill.

In the crucible of this rigorous life, the Mormon religion emerged. In that is its power.

In late fall of 1912, as the enlightened countries of Europe lined up for the First World War, Ebb Collard lined up two big horses with a makeshift wagon loaded with lumber and set out to such an historic stop – Steele's saw mill. He was on his way to civilization. He had camped in tents, lived in a cabin, and endured in a farm house. Now he set on one of his most liberating adventures. He would build his dream into an object and give it to God. He could not bring back the lives of the children, but he could move the promise of life forward. That's what he intended to do.

Although Jenny converted, he was not a Mormon. He had nothing against Mormons, he just distrusted religion in general. On that morning, just like the big wheel on the river, a mill wheel in his soul began to roll.

In the area surrounding the mill was a cleared field probably close to five acres. Once every twenty years or so, ice jammed the river and it flooded. When farmers plowed the field in the spring, they almost always turned up arrows and spearheads hand cut from flint presumably by the Erie Indians who lived there two or three hundred years ago. Closer to the river, one of Abner's cousins found a stash of spearheads including several made of obsidian, a rare stone only found in the Rocky Mountains. The only way that obsidian spear head could have ended up stashed in the Chagrin Valley is through ancient trade routes. Arrowheads. Spearheads. Spindle stones. A shard of obsidian. Such things, hallowed by magic and surrounded by mystery for perhaps 600 years, if not more, occupied Ebb's mind because these things were created by craftsmen like himself.

Elmer, his two sons, and the Hasseler boy waited for them at the mill.

Abner had known about this event for sometime. For the past few days, he had sharpened the mill blade with his best files and honed it with his finest stones. He made sure the gear mechanism that drove the long vertical blade up and down was lubricated and in fine working condition.

At the bottom of the hill, a covered wooden bridge, about sixty foot long, went over the river. The horses jolted and balked as they approached the bridge, but when the horses stepped onto the bridge they forgot the river. Donny ran across the bridge and took up a position to prevent any unsuspecting cars or wagons from coming through while the big horses began their passage over the river. The logs and the boards, secured by chains, probably exceeded the bridge's load limit. But Ebb, undaunted, sat high on the make shift wagon as it crept along. The bridge, supported by the steel girders, creaked and swayed just slightly. No one else was allowed on that bridge as he crossed it in faith praying for God's mercy.

Everything went fine – until they came off the bridge. Ebb turned sharply onto the last leg of the road to the mill. Without warning a wheel of the wagon slid on the gravel near a ditch, and the axle broke. The load shifted; the chain snapped, and the logs and boards broke loose. The horses neighed and bolted; Donny screamed, and Ebb cussed as he leaped to safety.

Hearing the commotion, Abner, Elmer, and some other fellows ran up the road from the mill where they found Ebb seated on the bank by the side of the road laughing.

Abner said, "It's a miracle that load didn't pull you and the horses *and the bridge* down into the Chagrin! Then you could have all floated down stream to the Mill."

"Miracle is about right for this!" he said.

"So this is that wood you've been talkin about all these years. That famous load of walnut and curly maple!" Abner said as he climbed onto the pile while Elmer steadied the horses.

"You're durn right. God's own wood! And I want that big log riff sawn to my exact instructions. That's why I brought it all to you." Ebb said as he stood up and brushed the dust off his clothes. "You're the only man in the county knows what I'm talkin about – at least half the time anyway."

Abner looked back at him with his head cocked sideways, as he stroked his beard, "I don't know if that's a compliment! But I'll take it as such."

"Well, we goin to find out today, that's for sure. I been prayin' about this venture since I was a kid!"

"Yes, we are! Good to see you Ebb Collard. Boy's, go fetch that wagon of mine from back by the barn! I want all this wood and this log on the mill floor in one hour. We got some mill work to do! 'This is a day the Lord has made! Let us rejoice and be glad in it!' " Abner hollered as the two men shook hands there in that steep and ancient valley amid the multicolored trees of late October.

At one o'clock, they gathered by the mill wheel, which was about ten feet in diameter. When they opened the sleuth gate, the water, no longer held back by a stone and gravel dam braced by timbers, came rushing through. It was an elegant symbol of man's harmony with nature. Ebb thought a photograph of that mill belonged on every household calendar in the world. He stood in awe as he watched it work like a good watch – steady, true, and faithful to the task for which it was designed.

All day long, the crew, who had camped together and hunted, who had planted and harvested, now sang songs as they loaded plank after plank and log after log on to the saw table. One song that stayed in their minds for a long time, went like this:

Come, come ye saints, no toil nor labor fear
But with joy wend your way.
Though hard to you this journey may appear,
Grace shall be as your day.
Tis better far for us to strive
Our useless cares from us to drive;
Do this, and joy your hearts will swell
All is well! All is well!

They sang that piece over and over as the wood slid into the edge of that tireless blade that rose and fell in a steady sweeping motion. Between songs, they told tales of the old days. Every cut was done in an exact manner. Ebb and Abner debated the best way to slice each board. They watched as the blade left long vertical lines. They were not like those arcs left by machine driven blades with high pitched *circular* saws. The vertical blade dated a board in the eighteenth century when men sawed by hand. But the rotary saw left a mark that placed the cut wood clearly as modern nineteenth century invention. Because of the vertical marks, the rough sides of these boards *would all look much older than they actually were.*

That evening, the happy and tired crew sat down on the porch at Abner's house. It looked over the river, which was about one hundred feet across with a depth above the dam of about fifteen feet. The lazy branches of tulip and maples trees hung their golden and reddish leaves over the river, which when reflected in the sunlight took on a glittering appearance reminiscent of ballroom dancers in flowing garments moving slowly. Ebb said, "Lovely place you have here, Abner. How long has your family been here?"

"Well, let's see, eighty four years since my grandfather came here. Yes eighty four."

"Never left. I can see why."

"Oh, some did. Yeah, some folks left with The Prophet in 1838. Others left with the Civil War. My father served three years with troops, and came back here with one arm. Lost his arm in the battle of Vicksburg in 1863. All those old fellas are dying off now. Why pretty soon won't be a Civil War soldier living. Wow, now there's a thought!"

"How did you father lose his arm?" asked Donny as he sat on top of a barrel on the porch.

"Well, son, he told that story many times. They was down on the edge of a swamp somewhere waiting for Johnny Reb to come up this road out of Vicksburg. He said mosquitoes were everywhere. They was layin' low right down in the muck getting ready for a surprise attack on the road, when low and behold a whole brigade come over a hill behind them not even knowing where they were. Both sides were surprised. They didn't even have time to turn the cannons around. They fired muskets, and then retreated up unto a ridge. Pop's unit got dispersed. He ran back into the woods. His arm bleeding where a ball caught it just below the shoulder. A kid probably fourteen or fifteen saw my pop squirrel up over some rocks. This kid yelled at my father to stop, but pop had a .32 caliber Cone pistol in a holster around his belt. Yes, indeed, pop waited for that kid to draw near him and he pulled up that pistol and fired at the kid who probably would have killed him. No tellin' what he would have done. Why, he hit that kid right in the knee. Yes, indeed, war's a nasty business, son. Pop said that kid squealed like a stuck pig. Cried for his momma. Then he staggered away before pop could get off another shot. Pop went over that ridge and caught up with his unit. They cut his arm off that night on a table in a tent. The only painkiller they had was a bottle of corn whiskey. He drank one half, and they poured the other half over the wound. He said years later at night he could still hear the sound of the saw slicing through bone and muscle. When they were done, he blacked out and woke up the next day miserable as the devil. He said that pistol saved his life. I still got it. Still works too."

By this time, Donny's eyes were wide as a full moon, and his jaw kind of dropped so he was almost speechless.

"I'd like to see that thing," said Ebb.

"Sure enough. Sit still, and I'll bring her here right now." Abner walked down to the Mill house and came back with a small box. He set it down on a table, opened it up, and pulled out a .32 caliber rim-fired, D. D. Cone long revolver with a hidden trigger. He popped some bullets into it and took aim at a can he set up on a fence post between the porch and river. He fired once and missed. Then taking aim, he blew the tin can into the air where it fell on the grass. "Still works!" he said. "Here, you try it Ebb. Only the best of my friends ever fire my pop's pistol. At this range she usually hits at about three o'clock. So don't focus right on target. It takes a while to get the hang of it."

They all took turns firing that pistol. It was a small thing that you could tuck in your belt and no one would see it. It was a family treasure without which, his pop may have never come back alive from the Civil War. The poor fellow died in 1894. He could swing a pitchfork with one arm, but could never steer a plow again. Throughout his life, he would wake up often at night screaming about the Rebs. He caught cold one winter while he was out setting traps, never did recover.

Now Donny took a serious interest in this pistol so much so that when Abner went to put it away in the Mill house, he followed along asking him questions about the war. They went into the saw room, which was not well lit. Donny watched as Abner placed the box with the pistol, just under the rafters. A small cabinet shop was built over top the sluice and the mill wheel.

"A pistol's a dangerous thing, son, a serious thing. I keep her in the Mill house just in case a bobcat or a wolf comes around."

"This mill is amazing. What does this *thing* do?" Donny asked as he stood in the dark watching Abner from the corner of his eye, all too carefully.

"That's a mill driven wood lathe, son. We will get her running tomorrow. I'll let you have a hand at it."

They went out, but Donny, who had a hankering for stealing knives and tools out of barns, had his mind set on another plan.

They slept in the house, some preferred to curl up right on the porch outside all night. In the morning, they ate breakfast on the porch at seven o'clock. During the meal, Abner said, "You know, I'm so glad about this adventure. I mean building a grand style cabinet for the glory of God, and not for gain of any financial kind is a way to get yourself focused. I want to stick with you fellas all the way on this. I'll tell you why. When the Mormon's built the Temple back in1836, which was before I was born, they were in their glory so to speak. They worked hard, but remained in unity and prayer believing they were preparing for the Latter Days, for the return of Christ. Of course, things never turned out as they expected. Still, the joy of working together for the community was so wonderful that losing the temple never seemed to matter. The true believers among them never forgot it. Never. It was simply one of the greatest things that ever happened in their lives."

"Well, you're surely welcome to pitch in and help," said Ebb, as he stood up and looked across the river at the golden leaves and ghostly mist that hung briefly over the slowing stirring river, "But I ain't no prophet."

"You said that before. But I know you're a believer in somethin' or you wouldn't be here now. Sometimes that's good enough."

They continued working for the next two day and then stopped near sunset.

Chapter Eighteen

A Snap of The Whip

During November, Ebb became preoccupied day and night with his project. Once he had the wood milled and cut to dimensions, he set a goal of thirty days in which to carve and join all the pieces. Working in that converted stable, all he had were hands saws, hand planes, and chisels and mallets. He did not like to work with soft wood like pine or even popular, but he loved his walnut boards. These were roughed in, and the drawer parts were cut down to one half inch stock at the mill. Ebb remembered when, as a young man, he began to work with hard wood and was surprised to learn that making a rough board flat on one side was perhaps his hardest chore. It required a good eye, a few sharp planes, and lots of muscle. Ebb now had the skills figured out for years, but the muscle, well, he had to renew that everyday. For that he needed help, and, thankfully, he did not have to work alone.

Elmer and his sons, along with Billy Hasseler came by about three days a week to work the boards. And Abner and some local cabinetmakers dropped by in the late afternoons and helped for a few hours.

Ebb, of course, insisted on his own layout work. He marked all the boards for width, length, and joinery; and handed them off for the others only after giving them firm instructions. Doing things this way allowed him to do his own carvings alone in the mornings or late into the night.

Donny, of course, was in and out of the shop in a jiffy. Working with his father made him nervous because he long ago learned he was more trouble than help. And he did not want to be yelled at or treated like an unruly child. So during this time, his wanderings were not without a devilish strategy. You might say he would have loved to work on the project, but not next to his own father who could become unbearable.

Donny had come to the time in his life when he felt he was growing up. But he did not recognize that his view of adulthood blinded him from seeing some most childish behavior. He had too much independence to be a child and too much rebelliousness to be an adult. Ebb, sensing this pressure, worried that something within Donny would snap like a whip, and he would end up being neither a child nor an adult, but a creature out of control.

One Wednesday afternoon he told his father that he had to run into town "*on an errand.*" He set off through the deep woods following a winding creek that ran behind Ware's castle. He made sure his route was unseen by anyone save for a few squirrels. As he advanced into the woods for about an hour, he kept looking back not for fear of being followed but to get his bearings for the return trip. When he broke out of the brush, he was right on the Chagrin about twenty yards below Steele's sawmill. He laid down in the grass and watched as people walked in and out of the mill and around the yard moving boards, and talking about their projects. The river was shallow below the dam. Probably knee deep at the deepest hole. It was about one hundred feet across to the mill, and yes, there was a watch dog who seemed to have a quiet place on the porch from which he surveyed everything.

Donny hunkered down there just like a Civil War scout making plans for an attack. After about an hour, he carefully crept back into the woods and followed the route by which he came, marking his trail by positioning rocks and branches in the stream, and studying outcroppings and oddly shaped trees that leaned over or had dropped across the creek years ago. He vowed to return on a night when there was no moonlight, following this same secret route, knowing that the route would be much more difficult on such a night.

When he came back to the house, Jenny had just set out the dinner table, and Ebb was back in the shop working on the carvings. "Did you help your father today?" she asked

"For a little bit. He kinda likes to do things his way."

"I know what you mean. When he concentrates like this, he completely loses sight of all his chores. That man can get so caught up in something. Perfectionist. Yes, just one way, and its his way."

"Yeah, well, I sometimes like to work with him, but then, every time I make a mistake or break something, he just starts that yelling of his: 'Why did you do it? Why didn't you ask me first?' I hate that."

"Well, he's your father, and he loves showing you things, but sometimes he gets jumpy."

"Why is he making that thing if he's not planning to sell it? Doesn't make sense? Pop never did anything wrong at the school. Doesn't make any sense!"

Jenny stopped in the middle of placing out the silverware and then she looked out the window as if searching for an answer to this question. "Well, Donny, do you understand what happened to him four years ago? About the fire?"

"Not exactly. That was a long time ago," he sat down at the table. "What happened?"

"Well, a year before that fire, your father and this Mr. Wilson were asked to fix the doors at that school house, and they got into an argument about how the door should open. Well, your father said once that it should open inward because the wind could rip it off. Wilson got mad and left. But after talking to some people and studying some drawings your father made it swing outward like they said. He made it open with an outward swing so kids could get out. But Wilson was not around to see it and did not care. Next year on Ash Wednesday when that school caught on fire, when the kids burned in that stairwell, people started saying it was your father's fault. But they were wrong about everything. All the doors opened outwards like they should, but the wind must have blown them shut. When those kids panicked and fell down in those crowded stairs, people never understood what happened. Some people, especially Mr. Wilson were mad at your father for setting the door wrong. They formed a mob, and they wanted to hurt your father. But there was no reason for it. Mr. Ware was worried so he helped us hide out here in the country until things were straightened out. Your father and I stayed out here in the country after that. That fire was just too much to bear. One hundred and seventy five kids burned to death, and sad to say, your father still feels he did it somehow. He wishes he could have done something more. Instead he just grieves."

"You forgot I was there, ma. On the third floor. Wilson's an old creep. He has a cabin up in the woods above the Sleepy Hollow Farm. I know where he hides out. I been there."

Jenny's voice changed as she looked at the boy. "Why, I believe he does live near there, but we never bother him any more. And don't you have no doin's with that man. He has a bitter soul. Why he lost his only son in that fire. He should never have tried to blame your father for what happened. It was all an accident. Your father did right by that door."

"So, we all suffer. I still remember that look on Mike's face on the moment when he fell into the flames," Donny stared straight ahead, talking in low tones, "So you didn't answer my question. Why's pop out there cryin' and buildin' a handmade cabinet for no money?"

"Abner Steele told him to do it as an act of atonement. It's his way of saying to everyone that he loves them. And that he loves their families, and he cares?"

"It don't make no sense to me. Old man Wilson was always a creep. He hated dad for some other reason. Somebody should bump that man off," Donny said.

Jenny turned around sharply, "Donny I do not want to hear you talk like that! Two wrongs don't make some thing right."

"I don't care. That man's been drivin' dad crazy for years. I know who he is. I remember Mike. He was one of my best friends. His old man comes here on weekends to hunt and burn trash and drink his beer with his ugly girl friends. Weird fella."

"How do you know so much about Mr. Wilson? And where you been anyway? And why are your pants and socks soaking wet? Look at you, looks like you been wallowing with pigs!"

"I been down by the creek checking traps for a friend from school. Just somethin' I told him I would do while he's out of town." The boy went on in a low tone, staring upward into space.

"Well get upstairs and change your clothes so we can have dinner before midnight. And don't be talkin so much about this Wilson. Lord knows your father hates the man. And don't be starin' into space like some sort of ghost. If you had any sense, you'd help your father."

Donny went upstairs to change clothes. This conversation had not been a good one for him. For the first time, he began to realize that this old school house fire, which he never understood, had a huge effect on his own life. It was why he lived in the country. It was why he was often alone. It was why his father was often angry and afraid. He began to realize while other kids had friends, he did not have anyone. He was a loner. Adults had failed.

He did not need their help now. He alone had a *plan* to set things *right. He could atone for everything*!

Chapter Nineteen

The Big Snow

Late in November of that year, it snowed – not that light fluffy snow that blew around like a frozen mist but rather an avalanche from on high. In a few hours the whole countryside was thrown back into the glacier age.

Early that morning, Ebb went back to his shop and stoked up his wood burning stove with some solid oak logs, then he lit a lantern, which he had surrounded by mirrors. He was now involved in placing his delicate inlay on the upper doors. The pieces that he cut from a stack of carefully aligned panels had to be arranged in a way that reflected their natural iridescence. Ebb mused that few woodworkers, even the experts, would know what he was doing at this point. He was beyond science, launched into an art that no one had documented nor discussed widely, if at all. Marquetry, as he understood it, was *next of kin to oil painting.*

While he concentrated in the warm shop, the boys, all of them, as well a few girls, had gathered around a steep hill above the valley, for the first big sled and snow ball party of the year. They brought their wooden sleds both store bought and handmade, and their snow boards made of solid wood. The older boys were anxious. They willingly rolled down a steep bank and tripped any unwary screaming younger kids who got in their way. So long as no one got hurt, it was the best of times.

Around noon, Donny did his famous Olympic leap. Taking a position high on the hill beside the large camp fire where the others came to re-cover from the cold, Donny stood up on a bobsled built for no more than three riders. Using his right foot like a kid's scooter, he advanced toward the steepest bank on the hill and dove over the rim standing all the way to the bottom. Just before the sled plunged into the frozen creek, he grabbed hold of a small cherry tree with his left arm and swung around as the sled went airborne. Hitting the ice with a loud crack, the sled spun around, undamaged. Everyone laughed and cheered for he was always the *grand performer* of death defying antics. His strength and agility and his deep need to gain attention always veered him toward the brink of self destruction.

"What did you hold back for!" Chris cried out from the hill top.

"Afraid of a little ice water?" someone else chimed in.

Rebuffed by the laughter, he hollered back, "Not one of ya could stand up all the way down without breaking a leg or arm."

"No one's that stupid! "

"Except you!" The laughter escalated.

Donny climbed down and pulled the bobsled out of the half frozen stream and brought it slowly up the hill challenging anyone to duplicate his feat. There were several who took his challenge, but none could handle the swift wobbly ride. They all fell in the snow. So all afternoon, he basked in his glory.

Around three o'clock, Abner and three other cabinetmakers came up through the woods astride big high-stepping horses jangling with bells. They had hunting rifles but no game. They were on their way back to Ebb's solitary place on the edge of the deep woods. They dismounted by the fire to warm their hands and feet and talk to the youngsters. Only one of them was foolish enough to take a ride down the slippery, ice coated hill that the boys had created.

Catching sight of Donny, Abner said, "Where's your old man? Out in that shop of his?"

"Probably. That's where he goes everyday."

"Good for him. I'm sure he's makin' somethin' beautiful back there." Abner said.

"Yeah, but not for money. He's just foolin' around back there. Piddlin."

"Son, we talked to the Lord about that. Your pop's a great man, and he's following the counsel of God himself. Yes, just as in the ancient days, he's a translator. That's the way I see it. He's taken a trunk of a tree and changing it into an expression of God's love. He's revealing God's handprint. We ought to all go back there and see what he's doin. See if we can lend him a hand."

"He don't like my help that much. I'm too wild with a blade or hammer."

"Son, I understand that. He don't like my touch either, and I'm good with tools. But you never know, maybe he just needs a person to support him in other ways with what he's doin. Why don't you come on back with us. Besides, might be some grub up there in the house. We've brought some venison and pork sausage with us. Homemade bread too. What do you say to that? "

"Sounds good. We been out here sledin' since breakfast."

With some reluctance, Donny went with them, the men on horses and kids following on foot.

They moved slowly, marching along the edge of an orchard. The horses hooves cut a path for their feet. The leafless trees had accumulated white edges of snow along the barren branches, even out to the ends of limbs, and in some places, even the thin wiry twigs were decorated with tiny ridges of snow which, given even a small puff of wind, would flake off and tumble like feathers in the crisp cold air. As they approached the farm they could see smoke winding above the chimney to the house, and back at the stable out of a dark metal stack, a column of silver smoke rose up slowly like a cloud and drifted toward the woods.

Out in the yard, they dismounted; and while some led the horses into the barn for a rest, the others took food to the house. Abner put his arm around Donny's shoulder and walked with the boy back to the stable, several straggled along behind throwing snowballs and laughing. When they opened the door they found Ebb so preoccupied that he had not heard them when they arrived. Soon everyone came in and filled the place. Ebb said, "Well, it looks to me like you folks been hittin the slopes out there by the orchard. Now how many of you fell in the creek this time?"

"Not me. But Donny swung out over the big pool on a cherry tree?"

Ebb looked around and laughed with the boisterous crowd that had broken in upon his solitude. Anyone near enough could see traces of tears in his eyes, which could have been from eye strain or most likely smoke in the air from his wood burner. Certainly not from grievin.'

"What you been up to?" Abner asked as he drew close and looked at the walnut board clamped to a heavy woodworking table. Chips from his cutting tools were scattered everywhere. There were chisels, small and large mallets, and all sorts of knives and stones to sharpen them.

"Oh, me. I've been carving the faces in the fire. One hundred and seventy five of them to be exact. I want them to be perfect. Each one."

"I'm sure they will be. But it seems to me these faces are out of the fire and into the heavens with the Lord. Praise God!" Abner said gently. "Yes, these here faces are glorified! The Lord's own kin! Folks what do you say we sing a song. It's cold back here and too quiet. Who has a song?"

"'Be still my soul', that's my favorite new song," said Billy Hasseler who looked at the fine carving while standing at Ebb's right hand.

"Wow, that's a tough one. Let's see if we can do it. Some one from the choir kick it off for us. I'm not good at that myself." And so they sang those words a little off key, some mumbling the words:

Be still my soul, the Lord is on thy side;
Bear patiently the cross of grief or pain:
Leave to thy God to order and provide
In every change he faithful will remain.
Be still, my soul, they best, the heavenly friend
Thro' thorny ways leads to a joyful end.

They applauded themselves and laughed together. "I don't remember the rest of the words," the choir member said.

"That was good enough just to put the music in our heads," said Abner.

"Sure needed that," Ebb said as he wiped his eyes. "You fellas bring any grub?"

"Soups on the stove up the house, so they tell me."

"Well let's get on over to the house. I've been at this all day. I'm hungry!"

As they walked ahead Abner dropped behind and gazed down the snow covered path that led to the river, "Atonement?" he thought. "Isn't that a process where a man reconciles himself to the Lord? What is happening here is way beyond that! Here is a guy speaking to the core of all of us while he carves faces on wood. He is saying, 'We cannot live in a state of self blame. We cannot allow God to blame us for what we are.' We need another answer. Now that's where atonement begins!"

And so it went all through that November. More of the same sort of thing followed. Marvelous things happened as Ebb, with the support of his friends, carved in his shop *atoning* for his sins.

Chapter Twenty

A Dark Winter Night

One would have thought, watching his father atone, might have been a source of celebration for the son, and perhaps it was. Yet two weeks into December, under the protection of a moonless night after a warm rain had abolished all the white snow, Donny made his own infamous "atonement" on the adult world as he understood it. On that night, he was, in his young mind, setting things right between God and man. He did a pretty nasty job of it. Some pent up anger, buried and hidden for years, twisted and warped by isolation, emerged as vengeance against a perceived threat.

It began at midnight as he dressed in a dark tight sweat shirt and dark pants and soft leather shoes that were perfect for running. He slept downstairs on the couch, since in winter, his upper room in the back of the house was too cold. When he was sure no one was awake, he slipped out the door quietly, and raced across to the stable where he found that black grease they used while hunting to mask their faces. He did not expect to be seen or caught, because no one would suspect such a crazy act as he was about to do.. His dashed across the field to the woods. This was perhaps the most daring part of his exploit; for once in the woods itself, there was no one foolish enough to be there at night. He had a big knife in a sheath on his belt.

The trip following the winding creek through the valley ran smoothly. It took about thirty minutes. He had no trouble finding the point across the river from the Mill on the Chagrin, but he was not prepared for the cold water. He waded across in ankle deep water that still had chunks of ice lodged against the rocks. Once on the other side, he moved along the gravel and sand bank quickly until he came to the mill itself where he stopped to take a breath and listen. He even paused to ask himself what he was doing and why. As he paused there with his back against the wall, he intensified his motives by thinking of all the years his father and mother had suffered over that school fire for which they had no more blame than anyone else. He himself had suffered but he was not able at his age to understand how or why God could allow such a horrible thing to happen. This hour of a private spiritual vengeance for all this suffering was near. The adult world had been wrong for centuries, and with a certain thrill and lust, he set his mind to complete the task set before him.

For a moment, pinned against that wall, he thought about abandoning the whole idea. Abner Steele was after all, a kind hearted man even though a little too meddlesome. The man and his family had grown up right here on the river. They knew everyone, and they were known by everyone as one of the founding fathers of the community. He had no grudge against them. But tonight was his night to send a message to the whole world. It would be an anonymous message. No one would suspect him and no one could stop him. With that thought before him, Donny saw beauty in what he was about to do. He was confident that he alone was about to set things right by his own devilishness. And so he ascended a ladder that stood against the wall and climbed over the rail and entered the mill room by sliding his hunting knife through the latch. His objective was one thing – that pistol in the box lodged up against the rafters. It was not theft that he had in mind, rather he wanted to *borrow* it for a while just to do a deed that *needed to be done*, and *only he could do it.*

Once inside, he moved swiftly across the room, removed the pistol and shells from the box in the rafters, and tucked the pistol into his belt, and filled his pockets with bullets.

He looked around, listened for any dog or human sound. He heard the water rippling over rocks in the river, far off he heard an owl in the woods, a mouse darted across the floor of the mill, a branch driven by a slight breeze scratched a northern window, and beyond these slight sounds, he detected nothing but absolute stillness. When he went out, the latch made a slight click. On the mill deck by the railing he glanced around before he went over the side, descended the ladder, and raced along the edge of the river where he paused, secluded in the safety of the woods. There, he loaded the pistol. No one person, not even a dog, had detected his presence. In a way, this was slightly disappointing. Everything was going way too easy.

His next pathway was not quite as familiar, so he proceeded a little slower as he was not sure just how many brooks and small streams he would have to cross before he would reach the right one. It took a little longer than he thought, but then again, he had neither a watch to keep time nor moon to guide him. He finally found the barbed wire fence that he wanted to find, and he was soon running down the dirt road that went along the edge of a field towards Stormy Wilson's secluded hunting cottage near Willowford. He knew the man would not be there, for it was the middle of the week. No one would ever know who did this.

He remained cautious, looking for car tracks, or a wagon, or a horse, but there was no one around. The pitiful one story cottage looked like a glorified chicken coup. He walked around it once before he began the assault. Then lifting the pistol and aiming, he began firing at the windows one after another blowing the glass into the building with each shot. He fired round after round as he circled with the Civil War pistol and saying somewhat loudly, "Take that you varmints! You swine! You tyrants!" Where windows did not shatter by the bullets, he picked up bricks off a stack behind the house and pitched them through the glass to complete the job.

When there was no glass left, he stopped and listened. Hearing nothing, he moved in closer to the building where he could see a mirror and some bottles and vases inside. He reached in with his right hand and fired at them shattering everything he could see. While pulling his arm out, he accidentally cut the back of his right hand on the edge of the glass, drawing blood. Quickly he pulled out a handkerchief from his pocket and wrapped the wound. Then he made five more shots into the ceiling and walls. He quit only because he ran out of ammo. The deed done, he backed away and laughed. "Here's to old man Wilson's stupid ugly face!" And he threw another big rock at the front door. He stopped. There was no need to proceed further. Far off he noticed a light at a neighbor's farm house across the field about a quarter mile away. That light was not on when he first came. A dog barked nervously there, and someone rummaged around out in the yard .

This evil deed was now a signature for the community. It marked the beginning of his justification for years of misery. He had avenged his family's humiliation He had just taught the adult world a lesson of his own, and it was time to run like a deer into the woods. There was no time to get back to the mill. He had to keep the pistol with him. He had not planned for this to take so long. But he could hide the pistol in the loft of his father's barn. No one would find it. He could take it back to the mill later. And so he took off

He ran and ran and ran for he could see over his shoulder now that someone had a car and was driving back that long dirt road toward the cottage. So he ran even harder until he came to a ridge, where he descended into the dark valley. At the bottom, he found a creek. He hid his trail by walking through that old wet creek for thirty minutes, until he came up to a valley below his father's farm. He paused and listened. He ascended the hill. At the top, he watched the smoke roll gently and innocently up from the chimneys. No one had followed him. He walked quietly across the field, entered the barn, climbed up in the loft, and hid the pistol in a small corner. He came down, washed his face and hands with a bar of soap and ice water, wrapped his wound with a bandage. He picked up some logs from the wood pile and walked to the back door of the house, as if nothing happened.

When he entered the kitchen, his father was there, half asleep at the Hoosier. "Oh, it's you," Ebb said. "Thought I heard something out by the barn. Where you been?"

"O, well, I scared off that raccoon. You remember that big one that's been comin' around, and then I picked up some more fire wood. Everything's fine. I'm goin back to bed. You okay?"

"Thought I heard gun shots, a long way off toward Willowford. That was about an hour ago. Did you hear anything?"

"Yeah, I heard that. Figured it to be someone trying to get rid of critters. You know how they try to get in your house in winter."

"Well, that was lots of shots for a critter. Get some rest. I'll probably go back to the shop now that I'm up. It's almost five in the morning."

Donny went back into the living room and laid down on a couch and pulled a wool blanket over his wet feet. His eyes were wide open as a big grin swept across his face. He could not sleep a wink. Now the deed could not be undone. Now, he could never escape from his victory that night. In his mind, he had sent the whole county a message that it would never forget. He knew that something had taken over his soul and compelled him to do what he did. At one level of his emotions, it was part of his fight for his satisfaction, for his sanity, for his justification before God and Man. On another level, it was part of his search for attention. At some deeper level, some wave length of emotions that moved like a violent quake under the surface of the earth, he knew even that night that this was only the beginning. A terrible sin, but he did not care, not on that night. He had spoken out.

As he tried to sleep, he imagined the look on the face of someone who drove back to that trashed cottage even now. He imagined the look that would come to the face of Old Man Wilson when he got the news; and even more, he felt the astonishment that would sweep through that man's soul when he found out how his thoroughly safe little retreat had been terrorized. Those people should never have made his dad suffer. He sent those evil gossipers a message with God's own pistol! He did what the adults wanted to do but could not. They were the cowards. He was the conqueror.

He must tell no one what had just happened. He would lay low now and be a good kid, *for this was Christmas*!

Chapter Twenty One

The Christmas Party

The week before Christmas, it snowed.

It was a gentle falling of windswept flakes that sculptured the fields, dashed around the barns and houses like playful kittens, and curled up the porches and eaves as if to sleep. That afternoon Ebb walked out in the yard, surveyed the clouds, and studied the winds by throwing handfuls of straw in the air and watching them blow around. There are many winter days when nothing much happens. The cold is tolerable, even enjoyable, and although the gray sky moves, it is not changing violently. At first, this appeared to be one of those. So he hitched old Finny up to the sleigh and set out for Willowford. He had arranged to meet Uncle Henry and his niece at the Interurban stop right in downtown. As he rode out he looked nervously around at the gray sky, the barren branches, and white fields; then, believing that he and old Finny could go where no automobile could ever hope to go, he snapped the reins, and she picked up to a brisk trot.

Meanwhile, Jenny and Donny prepared the house for a party. Elmer and his family and some friends, Alice and her son, Abner and his wife were all invited; and they would begin arriving in just about an hour. For years, the Collards, like any other family, had their own humble traditions, but this year was slightly different, for they had never in all their years, thrown a party at the farm house.

To prepare for the guests, Jenny placed a lot more green boughs about the house. They were on the mantle and the window sills, and even the table tops so much so the air was permeated with fragrance of pine. She hand painted pine cones and suspended them by red ribbons along the doorways. Wreaths made of grape vines and bright ribbons hung in the windows. Candles were discretely placed in metal holders so that they would not fall over and catch fire. In the fireplace, three big yule logs cut last spring from a fallen oak tree burned slowly. She had a fine spread of food: Cranberries, piccalilli, chocolates, and toasted bread, and several kinds of cakes and pies that she made while seated at her Hoosier cabinet.

Donny had cut down a pine tree and mounted it in a bucket filled with water, and decorated it with old heirlooms and new items. At the very top a star with a single candle waited to be lit on Christmas eve and not a day before. All day long, they worked at fixing things up. Now, as they waited for the guests to arrive, they tidied things up. They did not wait for gifts to be opened, for that would happen on Christmas morning. They would not exchange gifts tonight for that would be too costly for this humble home.

An hour after Ebb left, Jenny began to get nervous as she looked from the mantle clock over to the east window where she could see the road. "Do you think the roads will be too harsh for the automobiles?" she asked Donny.

"Nah, this is a light feathery snow, and I am sure Abner will come up from the valley on his sleigh with the big horses. They can pull out anyone who slides into a ditch. There is nothing to worry about except, of course, for pop."

"Why do you say that?" she asked in an agitated tone.

"The big hill that comes out of the valley could be slick. He just has Finny, and if someone else gets stuck, he could be in the middle of a mess."

"Goodness, you are right," she said as she looked once more between the clock and eastern window.

Donny put his hand on his mom's shoulder. ""Don't worry ma, pop can handle it. Everything will be fine." This Christmas, he had become unusually angelic with that small white bandage on the back of his right hand. He told everyone that he had cut his hand with the buck saw while he was out at the woodpile at night, and so they believed.

It was not long before the guests began to arrive. They actually all came together in one car that followed the sleigh drawn by two big horses that cleared and hammered the road with their powerful hooves. It was quite a regal entourage that entered the door. Their boots stamped the floor as they all laughed and pulled off their big jackets and shawls and caps. Donny hastily took everyone's wraps as he dashed up and down the stair to the bedroom like a court page.

"Some wound you got there on your hand, " said Elmer with a big smile on his red flushed face.

"A nothing. Buck saw slipped," said Donny.

"They'll do that if you let them!"

Daisy had a bright red ribbon in her hair, and Alice brought a huge basket with a smoked ham and sliced turkey.

"Oh, my there is way too much food here," said Jenny.

"And you folks will keep all of it!" said Alice. "I will not take one carrot stick back to the house!"

"That's right," said Daisy as they changed the subject before Jenny could catch her breath and protest against the charity. "Look at these beautiful decorations!"

Soon everyone strolled around and found their comfortable nooks in the crowded little house, and then the waiting began all over again.

There were many things they were not waiting for. They did not wait for the gifts because they had agreed not to do that. They did not wait to open Ebb's prize jug of homemade elderberry wine, even though it sat on a conspicuous place on the kitchen counter top. This was not an alcoholic party. Nor did they wait for the lighting of the top most candle on the Christmas tree for this was not Christmas Eve. No, this peculiar group had gathered in so far as they knew so that the simple joys of Jesus could be celebrated in the midst of this rather troubled house on the edge of the deep and lonely woods. There was a feeling, never exactly put into words, but always rumbling on the tips of thoughts that surfaced in the background of unspoken words – a feeling that as the years passed, this house had slipped deeper into the center of a pagan and eerie wood; that this group had gathered here to stop that retrogression of the Holy Spirit; that though they talked about everything else in the world, in the deep center of each heart, each of them prayed for a renewal of the Christmas spirit. And this was why they came here.

So that when they talked, it was what they did not say that seemed most bothersome.

Abner asked, "When did Ebb leave for Willowford?"

"It was about three thirty, wasn't it Donny?" Jenny said.

"I think so."

"Let's see it's just beginning to get a little dark," said Elmer.

"That's almost two hours ago," said Alice.

"Well, the roads are bad," said Abner. "Give them some time. They'll be here soon."

Then Jenny looked from the mantle clock and toward the east window which she now had to scrape with a wooden wedge because ice had formed on the inside of the glass.

"That valley hill's steep and slippery," said Chris.

"Ebb can handle it," said Elmer.

"Let's play a game of some sort?" said little Betty who was Chris's new friend.

Then someone laughed because they were all too silent.

"I'm not even worried!" said little Billy Hasseler in a most nervous voice.

Then, everyone laughed hysterically because the boy had made an admission which they all felt. And then more chattering began. After a few minutes, Jenny stood up and cupped her ear. "Listen!" she shouted. "Open the door, Donny! Listen, I hear the sleigh bells jangling on the harness. It's Ebb."

"It's them all right. That horse is moving at a good clip too!" said Abner as he opened the front door and stepped outside in the snow.

Ebb shouted and laughed as he pulled the sleigh into the driveway, and brought the horse to a halt. In those days, no automobile could go where a good horse loved to go. Men in the country still believed that you could not survive without a horse. Old Finny proved that tonight, as she jostled and stamped her hooves in the snow, obviously eager to run that whole track one more time

Soon, Ebb, Henry, and his niece joined the party in the living room as Donny took the horse and sleigh back to the barn. "Mighty brisk ride!" said Ebb as he jaws spread into a big and vigorous smile unusual for a man of such sobriety.

"You shoulda seen that Interurban. They let the coal fire burn out. It was freezin," said Henry the blind sage whose tall thin cane and dark glasses gave him the look of an ancient prophet.

Everyone spent a few moments getting reacquainted or in some cases introduced, then with a little guidance Henry found a chair by the fireplace where he warmed his feet. It did not take long for him to begin to pick on Ebb. "So tell me, Ebb, what you doin back in this woods? You used to be a city man, you know. What's this all about?"

"Well, I'm justa fool enjoyin my freedom."

"You don't say. Why this here room feels like an old log cabin. Just somethin about this fireplace that reminds of a cabin."

"Actually, the kitchen in back is an ole cabin, but this room here's a frame house built after the Civil War, so I been told anyway."

"I lived in a cabin, you know when I was a kid," said Henry as he rolled his head back and smiled. "I was glad to get out of it. But you, why you built some of the finest homes in Cleveland. How do you go from the finest homes in the city to the worst in the country? Who knows maybe you will retreat all the way to a tent. Oh, yeah, and then advance to a cave! Progress. Ebb's progress!" Henry started laughing and coughing so hard he choked on his own words.

Ebb laughed for moment and then he said, "You know I spent some of my finest hours sleeping with a few blankets right under the stars on a summer night! Aint nothin wrong with that either. Right up next to God himself!"

"Well, I'm not pryin into your life," said Henry as he rolled his head and smiled. "Just curious."

"Curious nothin, you pryin with every crow bar you can find!! I know you! An agitator! Not too sure why I brought you out here!"

"Now! Now! This here's the age of progress," said Henry as he swung his cane around to address his favorite nephew. "Do you realize men are flying in the air and racing down the road faster and faster everyday. Why that new Marmon car did seventy-five miles in a hour at the Indy race. Now that's somethin. Now I hear tell the new screw driven lathe can produce identical parts in the blink of eye. We got rail cars now that folks sleeps on! And then there's the light bulb itself. Manufactured right there in Collin Wood! And on and on it goes, but then we have Ebb, sleepin' under the stars with no tent even! What on earth is this about?"

"Freedom! I'm tired of makin' some rich man look good while I fight for survival. I prefer livin close ta the land!"

"Freedom! You call this freedom. You got to chop, you got to dig, you got to plant, and you got to harvest what you plant! That's farmin, that's almost slavery! You never get done, and you always die broke!"

"I do cabinetry, just like I did before in Cleveland. Rich folks from Cleveland are buildin big farms out this way. There's plenty to do," said Ebb as he stood up and leaned his elbow on the mantle.

"Have you got a Mill?" Henry said still smiling.

"Abner here has the best mill. A water-wheel mill down in the valley on the river."

"A water mill? Sure enough? Now we are talking antiques! Now what's this I hear about a hand made project you fellas been workin on. I'd like to see that one. You know, furniture been manufactured in this country for at least fifty years now. Why would someone make a hand made cabinet in the middle of the woods with no power tools. Don't make no sense! You could never make any money doin that."

Abner stepped forward at this point, sensing that the two men were reaching a sensitive subject for which he in part felt responsible, "Excuse me, if I might say a word here gentlemen. But I talked with Ebb about this for a long time now. He didn't do this for money. He did it for love. He did it for the love of God."

At this point, Donny was in the back of the room. He looked up at the ceiling while he ground one fist into the opposite hand as he tightened his shoulders. "Love, huh, that's a joke," he mumbled under his breath and laughed.

"Who said 'love' like that?" old Henry asked as he twisted his blinded head around.

"That's me Uncle Henry," said Donny. "Sorry, everyone, it don't make no sense. Buildin a fine cabinet in a rundown stable for love! Whose love? What's love?"

The room got silent for a second. Tension, which began in jest, now reached a crescendo driven by its own integral terror, as mixed emotions began to spiral. Ebb leaned on the mantel and stared at Donny and at Abner. The women and kids began to get quiet as they huddle behind the men fearful of an outburst. Clearly the father and son were entirely in disagreement about the meaning of this project. Abner began to realize just how much stress he placed on the family, but he could also sense the blind old sage was fishing around for some other reason. Maybe the old man was onto something.

Finally Henry stood up and smiled, "In the long run, love's the only thing that matters. I want to see this thing. I don't care how it's made as long as there is love. I got to feel it with my fingers. I want to touch it. If its got love, I'll see it with my soul, and I'll know it!"

"It's waitin for you out back," said Ebb as he slowly pulled his arm off the mantle and gave his son a mean look. "We'll talk about love later."

"I know it is. That's why I came here."

The men and boys began pulling on their coats as just about everyone sensed a certain disarray had taken over the whole party.

"Oh Lord help us!" said Jenny. "Whatever is goin on with this party.? We were just about to spread the food out on the table. Can't this wait?"

"Honey, we won't be that long. I just want to show'em somethin' then we will come back and have dinner. That's all just show'em somethin'."

Soon they were out in the snow which was not deep, just up to their ankles. The wind had eased down to a few random puffs. They walked in pairs extending the same debate. Donny trailed behind, making a snow ball and throwing it at the other boys. They talked about techniques and prices, about self expression and the abuse that comes from shoddy products built by the factories, about freedom and the lack of it. It was an old discussion, not often about wood working and tools, but always about the meaningful expression of one's self. The word freedom was a line drawn in the snow. None could agree on what it meant, but everyone knew how it felt.

Once in the shop, Ebb pulled the doors closed. He had a wood burner in the center of the room. There was a frail glow of the last embers in the hold so he threw in a handful of kindling and one modest piece of oak, and then closed the door firmly. Some of them walked around looking at Ebb's benches and tools while he went about lighting several lanterns that had shining mirrors to reflect the light. Quietly, over the jokes and the mumbled ends of conversation, Henry said, "Listen!"

They stood still and listened as the women sang while someone hammered a dulcimer:

> Silent night! Holy Night
> All is calm! All is bright. ...

Henry said, "You need not light those lanterns for me," said Henry. "I've seen hand tools before!"

The others laughed. Ebb walked over where a stall once stood and reached up and pulled a big gray canvas off a tall object. He said, "It's been a long time comin, but I wanted you all here for this moment. So they gathered around as the lights threw golden accents over the waxed and shiny cabinet. The great secretary was done. Down her front door there was a cascade of marquetry and carving fit for the finest king. Around her feet, there was a rippling line of elegant molding, and on her top, a tapered and coved crown.

"By golly, you did it!" said Abner as he drew near with a hushed voice.

Ebb opened the slant front top and held up a lantern so that they could see the intricate work hidden in the interior much like gems in a jewelry box. He pulled out one of the small drawers and handed it to Elmer, and said, "All this was handmade. A life time of dreams, and seven years of getting ready for the final joinery, and thanks to you folks, done in about forty days."

Henry came in closer, "I want to feel the carving on the drawer fronts. I remember the drawings from years ago. I want to feel the carvings. In my mind, I'll see them. Just let me feel those carvings."

The voices came clear from the house:
> *Silent night! Holy night!*
> *Shepherd quake at the light.*
> *Glories stream from heaven afar!*
> *Heavenly hosts sing hallelujah!*

Just then, a mysterious thing happened. Old blind Henry, frail as a reed, reached up and turned the cabinet door back with a soft trembling touch, just like some priest swinging a pot of incense in a temple. His blind eyes squinted while he rubbed his fingers over the marquetry; and then in a hushed whisper, as if remembering something beyond the comprehension of anyone in the room, as if he were in a another world listening to a drum distinctly different, a soft drum embellished with laughter in an unusual rhythm beaten on a hide that had been harvested out of primeval brush in a distant land; a sound fitted for this world's most intricate designs by the mind of a God that extended from the core of reality to the delicate interior of the human heart, and he said softly: " The Kola Dari is here."

Abner whispered, "What did he say?"

Elmer said, "I'm not sure."

And the man whispered it again, " Kola Dari!"

Abner said, "Kolob, that's from the pearl of Great Price!'

Ebb said, "He's talkin about my great grandfather, a London cabinet maker who designed this piece over a century ago. I never knew what the word meant but it was on the drawings."

"Why it refers to the bright star where God watches over all creation?" said Abner

Henry said softly, "It means *the hand print of God,*to the Iroquois. I can feel God's hand standing here. You did it Ebb, you built the Koladari. God put his print in the wood, and you brought it to life. What I see here and now is a pure heart. You did this one for love."

They all watched as the old man rubbed his hands over every piece of that cabinet. None of them had seen anything like that. It was as if the cabinet itself talked to the old man telling him where it came from, and how it evolved through nature into its present form.

"Praise the Lord, it's the Kolob-dari!" said Abner.

"Let's go get the sleigh and take it up to the house," said Ebb as he went out. Donny went out behind him. They both stood outside for a moment still as stone. They listened to the women singing another hymn. Tears came to Ebb's eyes as he stood there with his hand on Donny's shoulder.

"Son," he said, "I'm sorry for all the wrong things I've done to you and mom over the years. I hope you understand this moment. It's not some selfish love. Not at all. This is about listening to God. For me, I ain't good at speakin through words, but woodwork, that's all I do. I just had to do this. That's all. I don't know exactly why."

"Pop, I got something I have to confess to you. Maybe not now. Maybe later."

"That's okay son. Tell me later. Right now, I'm flyin' like an eagle . I can't believe I did this. Now that I did it, I've got to become a prayin' man. I've got to humble myself. God expressed himself through me. I been baptized just like your mom was, right in the river of this shop. Your welcome to join me, son."

"Ah, well, I may have to do some serious praying about that one, pa."

More of the same celebration took place in the living room where they brought the secretary and set it up next to the Christmas Tree. It was too tall and too lavish for that humble house. Everyone was astonished by the minute attention to detail and the iridescent glow of the wood itself.

Jenny said, "Gracious me. All the tears that went into this!"

"I made her in the old way. Dovetail and Mortise. Hand planed every board. The few nails that are in it are probably over a hundred years old. Everything about it is old. Why, someday someone might think it was built before 1800. Well, I did that because it's God's own way. Wood's supposed to hold itself together. Don't need these modern glues and gadgets. None of that plywood stuff will last. She ain't a gas balloon. This will last five hundred years. Yes indeed. "

Part Three
Resolution

Chapter Twenty Two

The Revelations At The Inn

At six o'clock back at Reed's Inn on the day of Susan's antique sale, the phone rang. There was only one person there. Mary was the bartender. She was an older person, that is, old enough to be someone's grandmother, and yet, beneath her slightly gray hair which curled over her forehead in a fashion reminiscence of the fifties, young enough to hold her own with a room full of rowdies. The lines on her face were engraved by the dry sun, and each of her swollen knuckles showed the onset of arthritis. A cigarette hung from her dry red lip as she wiped the bar top. When the phone rang, she crushed the butt into an ashtray until it was formless trash.

"Reeds!"

"Hello? Is this Reeds Historic Inn in Kirtland."

"Yeah. It's all the same. You got the bar in the back because nobody's up front. How can I help you, honey?'

"Is this the same Reeds where they have the antique auction?"

"Yeah, there's been some bunch like that around here all day. Some sort of fancy eastern folks. They said they was comin' back at six thirty, but we will wait and see about that. We usually close at seven."

"Is there a person there called, Susan Robbins?"

"Yeah, that's the blond lady with the fancy shoes! Supposed to be runnin' this thing. She said she would be back at six thirty, but like I said, we close at seven, and they don't pay me no overtime. I mean I can hold the bar open for a little while, if there's tips in it. But I ain't supposta. If you know what I mean."

"Well, can you pass a message onto her from me?"

"Sure, wait till I get a pencil. My memory ain't so good. Hold on, jesta sec. Okay shoot?"

"Well, this is Sister Emerson from the Church of Jesus Christ of Latter Day Saints, and I need to speak to her right away."

"That's a lot a words. Hold on honey. Pencil just broke. Okay, I found a pen. Sister who?"

"Sister Emerson."

"Okay, and the Church."

"Yes, The Church of Jesus Christ of Latter Day Saints."

"Hold on now. Just writing slow here so she can read my hand writing. Okay. Is this an emergency?"

"No, but I must see her. I will be there with some friends at six thirty. It's very important. I have been sent there by my grandfather, a Mr. Hasseler. Please tell her I will be there."

"Okay, honey, is there anything else?"

"No. Please tell her it is terribly important that she see me."

"I'll give her this myself."

"This is about a revelation. But well, ...I'll explain that when I get there."

"Thank you, honey. Take care now. Goodbye."

"Thank you. And may God Bless you."

"Same to you, honey."

Mary hung up the phone and kept scribbling nervously. She pulled up her reading glasses which were suspended on a silver chain around her neck, and continued to write down as much as she could remember. "Did she say reservation or revelation?" Mary said. She went back to work leaving the half scribbled message on the bar by the phone.

About fifteen minutes later, the cars began pulling into the parking lot. People got out and talked and laughed outside. Soon, they began to filter into the dining area. Some whispered quiet and secret words as if they were involved in a conspiracy. Some came straight back to the bar and ordered some drinks, but without a word, turned and left for the dining room. Paul and Susan came a little late. They rushed from the front door into the dining area. Susan looked nervous and disheveled as if she just parachuted out of a wind storm.

Mary looked up from bar and saw two young girls and an elderly man and wife come in looking a bit lost. Suddenly she remembered the phone call and the note and went across the back way to the dining area where she found Susan and Paul talking with Crandall.

"Excuse me, Mrs. Robbins. Listen there was a phone call for you earlier. I believe that might be your party right over there by the door."

Susan looked at the note and folded it in her hand, "It's some new people. I wonder if Hasseler made it?"

"Here we go again," said Paul.

Crandall tightened his necktie in a peculiar way as he raised his eyebrows and caught the attention of the man with the big gold ring who stood across the room. He moved his lips in manner that expressed his unspoken words, as if he said, "Hasseler's people." Bob Harper caught the message clear across the room, and excused himself as he came closer to the secretary. The whole atmosphere then changed as the young women and the elderly couple were now face to face with the secretary itself.

Then almost instantaneously everyone hushed as they gathered around the secretary eager to hear what was being said. Susan raised her hands in the air and asked everyone to be silent. "Can we bring back the folding chairs and have everyone be seated please. We have guests here who have been sent by Mr. Hasseler, and they wish to make a statement. I have no idea what this will be about. Let's wait and listen."

Chairs were placed in order quickly as the group laughed and whispered with excitement.

After a few minutes, Susan introduced the new arrivals, "This is Sister Emerson and Sister Lovelace, and Elder Cartwright and his wife, Sister Cartwright. These are missionary representatives sent here at Mr. Hasseler's request. They are stationed at the Kirtland Historical Sites of The Church of Jesus Christ of Latter Day Saints. Sister Emerson will share information from our friends. Sister."

Sister Emerson stood up. She was a tall young woman about twenty one years, with short blond hair neatly combed. She had ruddy cheeks that glowed with her exuberant smile. Her dress was beige, plain, without embroidery of any sort. Her shoes were remarkably plain, brown rounded forms fit for mountain climbing. But something about her was radiant. She began talking nervously. "We know that we do not have much time this evening, and yet there are a thousands words we wish we could tell, but we must be brief. First, thanks for having us here. My grandfather wanted to come himself, but fell ill on his way to the airport. He is in the hospital, but he is all right. His son is with him. Second, we are missionaries and as such, we are obligated by strict rules of our church to share with you the restored gospel of Jesus Christ. So if you do not mind, we would like to begin with a prayer. I'll ask Elder Cartwright to offer that."

The old man in a black suit with neatly trimmed gray hair rose to his feet and folded his hands behind his back as he spoke with great force and brevity. "Our Heavenly father, we thank you for this moment, for this Inn, and for these fine people who have gathered here, and we thank you for the Scriptures. Please watch over and heal our dear friend Jeffrey Hasseler and help us to convey his message this evening. In the name Jesus Christ, we ask this. Amen." The man smiled and sat down.

"As an LDS missionary, I must share scripture with you. I apologize if that offends some, and actually it makes me nervous. But what I will read here is relevant to the origin of this secretary, if indeed this is the secretary that my grandfather remembers. I 'm reading from "The Pearl of Great Price", the book of Abraham, Chapter 3. These are inspired words translated by the Prophet Joseph Smith from certain (and I quote here) "ancient records that have fallen into our hands from the catacombs of Egypt." I will begin reading with verse 2:

> Abraham saw the stars, that they were very great, and
> that one of them was nearest unto the throne of God: and
> there were many great ones which were near unto it:
> And the Lord said unto me: "These are the governing
> ones; and the name of that great one is Kolob, because it
> is near unto me, for I am the Lord thy God; I have set this
> one to govern those which belong to the same order as
> that upon which thou standest."

She stopped, closed the books and said, "May God bless the reading of these words. Amen.

"My friends. I have here a copy of a photograph taken in February of

1914 at the Grange Hall in Kirtland, Ohio. In this photograph, you find a man named Ebeneezer Collard, his wife, Jenny, and behind them a group of people called the Kirtland Cabinetmakers. The cabinet in front of them is very similar to the one standing before you just now. Sister Lovelace will pass these copies out to anyone who wants one. According to my grandfather, this cabinet was known affectionately as 'The Kolobdari" which meant that it was blessed because it revealed the hand print of God. The wood was carefully chosen. The design thoughtfully put together. The purpose and intent were pure.

"The name, "Kolobdari", was not a whimsical word. The name Kolob comes from an ancient expression designating a planet or place where God dwells. The Source and Creator of All Life, God wants us to draw near to him. As found also in the book of James, Chapter 4, when we draw near to God, he will draw near to us. Ebb Collard was a man deeply depressed and angry at the world for certain misfortunes. He had been blamed for making the doors on a school open inward. As a result 175 victims were trapped in a school on March 4, 1908. He did not put the doors on incorrectly. As is well known, the doors never opened inward. They had to be pushed out. But tormented by these accusations, he fled to the country where he became friends of a small group of Mormons. These people were all cabinetmakers and farmers. At some point they advised him to build this cabinet by hand in the old manner and in the wilderness, and that they would help; and if he did that in prayer and humility and not for any financial gain, he would be blessed. Today we call such things therapeutic art work

"According to my grandfather, he built this cabinet in forty days, and he was blessed. Unfortunately, the cabinet had to be sold to pay for damages to another man's house. So the maker never got a cent for it. But he became a witness to the Mormon faith until his passing in 1926, and he was known as a joyous song leader.

"Now, I know you all want to know how can I prove this bizarre story. I see it in your faces. I hear your grumbling. You are making me very nervous." She laughed and so did the group. "But hey, I can handle that! I'm a missionary. My grandfather has given me a list of questions to ask. And I am going to go through these quickly because if he was here this is what he would do. First, has anyone here found the secret drawer? Because it will say that what I have just told you is true. Did anyone find the names?"

Paul Robbins stood up and smiled, "Sister Emerson. Thank you for coming here. I really appreciate this. This is amazing. I am not a Mormon, so I am unfamiliar with that scripture. I'd like to check into that later. I gather that you are a messenger for someone else. But you have no idea what we went through today. We have torn this cabinet apart more than once, and we cannot find a name or date anywhere. We did find a secret drawer, but nothing was in it. It's our opinion that the date is probably much older than you're saying. This photo doesn't actually change our opinion. See it's kind of old and blurry. So my answer is: we found a drawer but nothing was in it. So the answer is no."

"Thank you for sharing that. Now, please bear with me. I am not myself an expert on any of this. First, please tell me where that secret drawer was located? Could you please show me that drawer."

At this Elder Cartwright stood up and said. "Excuse me, but it is possible that this cabinet is not the one we are searching it for. You see, we are on a mission here for Mr. Hasseler. The Kolobdari was a sacred artifact to him and his family. He looked for it all his life, and this may not be it."

"Oh, no problem, Elder Cartwright. We want the truth too. I'll take that secret drawer out for you." Paul said and raised his gloved hands in the air and walked up to cabinet. He pulled down the slant front, removed one drawer, and then the small one behind it. "Here it is! That's all we found. Nothing carved or written on either of these drawers."

Sister Emerson examined it and said, "If you don't mind, Paul. Can Sister Lovelace take a photograph of the drawer, you are holding? I'm sorry but these are my grandfather's instructions. He is very serious about this."

"No problem. After today, I understand why you are asking this. Believe me!" said Paul holding the drawer in one hand and pointing to the spot from which it came. The digital camera flashed two or three shots.

"Now I need a ladder and I have brought with me a long screw driver."

"We have the ladder here," said Paul as he began positioning the ladder.

Crandall came forward nervously. "Now, young lady, you must stop this immediately. You must tell me what you intend to do because I am the

official protector of this asset. I guaranteed it against damages and alterations by anyone. These two people, Paul and Susan own it. But I protect
it."

"Thank you, and your name please."

"Crandall Armes, professional curator. Here is my card!"

"Thank you, Mr. Armes. My grandfather has given me these instructions for obtaining permission to examine another secret on this cabinet.
Will the owners please stand up before the entire group? Please tell me
your full names."

"Susan Lillian Robbins."

"Paul Ernest Robbins."

"Thank you for that. This is what I intend to do. I will first release the
finial at the top center of the cabinet. I will insert this screwdriver in the
finial hole and it will release a locking device. Then carefully, that entire
molding should slide upward, and behind it we will find this secret drawer.
We have some idea what it will say there, but keep in mind, no person
living today has ever seen what is in that drawer. Do you Susan and Paul
Robins give me permission to attempt to reveal the contents of this secret
drawer."

"Absolutely, " said Paul.

"Of course, Crandall if you don't mind!" said Susan. "I knew something
like this was coming. There are reasons."

Crandall flushed with pure unadulterated rage. His face turned red as
he sat down. "Have it your way," he said.

"If you don't mind," said Paul. "I'll perform the task itself. I will even
wear the white gloves," he said as he pulled on a fresh pair. As he spoke,
he climbed the ladder and performed each task, "I am removing the finial
which has a set screw to hold it. Here take that. I am now inserting the
screwdriver into a slot that is at the base of finial hole. It looks like a pilot
hole. I am turning it clockwise. It's a little stiff but it is moving something.
Some sort of lock. The molding here is now free. Amazing! It is sliding upward on wooden dowels. My Gosh. There it is. Underneath. Let me pull
this plywood panel out. There it is. It says,

'Built by E. Collard and the Kirtland Cabinetmakers,
December 1912. In Memory of those Who Died at Lake

View School, March 1908.'

And here on the back is something called a "Roll Call" with the names of the children, written in ink on a burnt plywood board."

Expressions of astonishment filled the room as Sister Lovelace took a photograph of Paul while he held up the board on the ladder.

"Well, it sounds like our date is correct," said Sister Emerson. "Now the reason that we knew this was true was because William Hasseler, my great grandfather bore witness to the carving, and the insertion of this secret board, and he was asked by Ebb Collard not to tell anyone. That hidden board by the way came out of a door on the school. We believe that the builder wanted no glory, no credit, and he wanted the names hidden. It was too painful, plus, for some reason he disliked plywood. We do not know why."

By this time, most were awestruck. Susan began trembling, and Paul became excited because he, like just about everyone in Northeastern Ohio, knew something about that tragic school fire, where kids got to the doors.

As Susan's wept, her mascara slid down her cheeks. Her whole body trembled. She choked on her own words. "I'm sorry, "she said. "But, ever since I first arrived this morning, I felt something like this would happen. In fact, I've always felt chills from the moment I found it in that attic. I just can't believe the extent of what you just said. Thank you so much for coming here today. I'm speechless. I have ancestors who died in that horrible fire. So, I can't say any more."

Seeing her shaken, Paul came over and gave her a supportive hug. As he held her closely, he murmured some uncharacteristic consoling words, then he raised his voice and spoke to all present in the room. "I would like to say a few words to everyone. I'm deeply sorry for my rude jokes this morning. I'm sorry if I made it difficult for my wife to express her insight. But, as I stand here now, I am beginning to see what this is about."

Then holding his wife's hand, he walked up to the door and defying all protocol, he touched the carvings with his fingertips. He felt an electric tingling as he tenderly drew his fingers over the sharp incisions made by a delicate chisel. Hundreds of these markings. Each was a voice. A scream. A groan. Each child spoke from beyond this world. "This man who did this..." Paul paused as he pressed both hands on the carvings, "I feel it now. Whoever he was, whoever made this – this man was there at the door on that dreadful morning. He saw those faces dying before his eyes. He felt the heat. And not once, mind you, but over and over in his memory. This is why he built this. It's not just another secretary desk, but an expression of his anguish and his hope. Our hearts have been embittered and hardened by the age in which we live, so we need to pause for a moment before we can understand what he did here."

Paul closed his eyes as he guided his hands over the carved surface. Little did he know, but he felt the same message Uncle Henry felt ages ago.

"But look! Look for yourself at these delicate carvings. Better yet don't look just come here and feel it. This guy felt a glorification of life beyond words. Perhaps, we can never be sure, but I sense he felt this whole thing was his fault. This humble guy. This unknown face in the crowd. This anonymous cabinetmaker. Whoever he was, he was there at the school door on that day, and I can feel something else. Feel it for yourself! I could be wrong, but this guy put a face on God Himself. What we see here is God lifting those school kids out of the flames and transporting them to paradise."

As he spoke, everyone drew near to touch the faces.

Paul went on with his soliloquy. "You know, I'm a mechanic. I fix cars. But I could be wrong, but I think not. This guy may have built the door that trapped those kids. When you build a door, you have two choices. Build it so it opens freely or build it so it closes firmly. He may have built a door that closed too firmly, either way. He got into trouble. In some sense, we are all like him. Closing one door, opening another. That's the story of life. I may have been a thoughtless person at times, but I think this guy was tormented by something he did at that doorway. You know, God himself built a set of doors called life. We only have so much time, and then there's that opening of the final door. Open them carefully, my friends, close them gently, for the faces we leave in the fire will never go away!"

Susan closed her eyes and pressed her hand against the carved surface. "Yes!" she said as if vindicated, "*Yes.*"

It took a while for everyone to leave that evening.

Chapter Twenty Three

The Epilogue

School kids. That's what this story is about. That's why the secretary was built. Kids all over the world. Their aspirations. Their dreams. Their energy. Their young community is their own place, not ours. Their community cannot belong to the adults that provide it. We cannot own them. We can only provide a safe place in which they can begin to claim their own destiny. They cannot be asked to provide a place for themselves. If for any reason their basic safety is not provided, we are responsible for the consequences. When they suffer excessively, our future collapses.

This is why we remember March 4 of 1908. At the Lake View School in a building built by adults, the kids did as they were told. They followed the rules, and yet they were entrapped. Shortly after that fire, all public schools in the country came under scrutiny. None were allowed to have narrow, crammed exits. All doorways had to have mandatory panic bars that opened outward. The structures were to be built of steel, stone, and concrete. The lighting had to the best available. Many other safety measures which we take for granted today came into being after that small holocaust.

Kids and fires. The scars are many. The wounds deep and lasting.

And yet, somehow the beautiful must rise out of ashes. We, the living, may never understand how a dreadful thing can be transformed into beautiful. But we have no choice in the matter. We must rebuild with a generous and forgiving heart. Old grudges, errors, and omissions cannot become excuses for blaming a scapegoat. According to Scriptures, we must forgive not seven times, but seventy seven times. This is never as easy as it sounds. A few years after that horrible catastrophe, the community changed radically. There was a new fire resistant school built south of the old building, and a memorial garden built on the foundation of the old school. Community programs to help those who suffered were numerous. In spite of casualties, Collin Wood became a better place.

Our fictional character, Ebb Collard, suffered for the rest of his life from post traumatic stress, a serious psychological illness found in every village on the planet. But thanks to the community and his own efforts, he learned to understand and manage it. Eventually, he sold that beautiful cabinet to pay for damages to Jim Wilson's cottage. Jim and Ebb reconciled most of their differences and settled that matter. Donny did some jail time, before he moved onto the battlefield in World War I. Not long after it was sold, the cabinet vanished into a home where eventually, after fifty years, the final owner never knew where it came from. The town of Steele's Mill survived up until the nineteen thirties where it failed during the Great Depression. At that time, the last members at of The Community of One Church merged with another group and forgot the old stories of the past. After World War II, strange, new people moved into the valley; these folks drove around in faster cars, watched moving pictures on flashing tubes in their modern houses, and knew very little of the previous generations. But all their stories belong in other books yet to be written.

Fiction, such as it is represented here, allows us to look a little deeper into our own hearts. If we do this intentionally and with the appropriate devotion, the underlying truth of history will become clearer to us, in as much as we can know it at all.

www.ingramcontent.com/pod-product-compliance
Lightning Source LLC
Chambersburg PA
CBHW030326020726
47493CB00004B/1177